Savage Seas

Savage Seas

by: Brigit Rosé

Copyright © 2024 by Krystyna Fenner

All rights reserved.

Published by

Two Realms Publishing LLC

https://tworealmspublishingllc.com

Book Cover: We Got You Covered Book Design

Interior Design: Two Realms Publishing LLC

Editor: Ink It Out Editing

ISBN: 978-1-955106-41-2

Printed in the United States of America

Savage Seas

Brigit Rosé

Warning

This book is full of foul language, lots of death, and not enough smut in my humble opinion. That doesn't take into account the light stalking, a bit of domination, backstabbing, the alphaholes, a possessive MMC, and a fiery FMC, both of whom are determined to blow shit up.

So, I hope you're good with pussy and the endless use of fuck. It occurs 117 times in this story in several variations. Yes, I counted. According to my mother, my characters need to learn a new word. I disagree. As for the smut, it's there, and a decent amount. The characters and I argued over how much.

As this takes place in my NYC world, you'll cross paths with shifters, vampires, hunters, and witches. And the main guy, well, he's a merman who has a knack for charring his victims and a shoot first, ask questions later philosophy.

If that doesn't wet your palate or it offends you, then this book may not be for you.

Continue at your own risk.

Chapter One

Gray peered through the rifle scope, sighting his prey. Hitting his target this way was a bit on the antiquated side, but the male didn't travel alone. He spotted his victim in the passenger seat of a black van as it pulled into the dimly lit parking lot. At least he didn't need to lure the male to the dock. The guy had arrived all on his own. Though it certainly took away the thrill of the hunt. He rather enjoyed that look of fear that filled every one of his victim's eyes when they realized death had come for them.

While he wouldn't get up close and personal with this target, he'd still revel in the kill. After the mess the male and a few others had left in the waters last week, they deserved nothing less. He ensured that everyone who crossed his...family...suffered at his hands.

The black van parked in a spot not too far from the dock's entrance. He watched as the driver and his target climbed out of the vehicle. Although he could strike from this distance, he didn't want to take out his prey too early. Where would the fun in that be?

His gaze narrowed as the two men strode around to the back of the van and two more men got out. The four lingered there for a moment, discussing something. Not that he could tell what from his position in the tree. What the hell were they doing?

"Just grab her!" his target yelled.

Her? Shit. Didn't that just complicate matters? Eh, only a little, the more he thought about it. He'd let things play out, not that he'd let them go too far. It might even give him the opportunity to end more than one life, drawing no attention to his pod. His leader wouldn't like that.

Two men lifted a dark-haired female out of the back of the van. She squirmed, struggling against their hold, and shrieked through the gag around her mouth.

"Shut it, Red!" his prey hollered. "You brought this on yourself."

It didn't matter why these men intended to harm or kill the female they carried. He could easily save her with a headshot to each male in a matter of seconds. His finger inched closer to the trigger, settling against the cool metal. One move. That's all it would take.

They'd easily drop her. What if she got hurt in the process? Or she got caught in the crossfire? Maybe he just needed to wait until they got closer. Then he'd take less of a chance that the woman got injured. Gray shook his head. Why the fuck did it matter how he saved her? Or if she got a little banged up?

Shit. He didn't even have to save this chick. It wasn't his primary objective. The bearded guy was the only one left of the group to kill. Gray scrubbed a hand across his face. Saving the chick came second to that. The how mattered little. His gut twisted at the mere thought of her getting hurt.

Fuck. What was wrong with him? He needed to get it together. Steeling his shoulders, he looked through the rifle scope. Son of a bitch. He'd lost track of them. It shouldn't take him long—they'd moved faster than he expected.

Only one man had a hold of the female now. Gray narrowed his eyes as the male's grip tightened on her. His target removed the woman's gag. "Tell me where it is, Red."

"Fuck you!" she spat.

"Wrong answer." His prey backhanded the woman, splitting her lip.

A low growl rumbled in Gray's chest. One tiny squeeze and he'd explode this piece of shit's head. Though if he waited a few more seconds, then he might just find out what they wanted. Either way, this shitbag was about to die.

"Shh," the male holding the female demanded. "Someone's here."

Gray stilled his body, leveling his breaths so they blended with the gentle breeze. New York City was so cold this time of year, it took extra work to camouflage with the background. No way they could hear or see him.

His target swiveled his head around, scanning the surrounding dock. "Ain't no one here but us." The male frowned and turned his attention back to the woman. "Now, let's try this again. Tell me where it is, Red, and we'll make this quick."

With a gleam in her honey-brown eyes, the corner of her mouth upturned. "Might as well kill me now, Chucky, because I'll never tell."

"Don't call me that!" He struck her across the face, jerking her head to the side.

It took every ounce of control he had not to react. His entire body itched with rage. He wanted to race down there, wrap his hands around that grubby bastard's neck, and squeeze the life out of him as he sent endless jolts of electricity surging through that shitbag's body.

Her tongue snaked out to the corner of her mouth as she focused back on the male. "What's the matter, Chucky? Don't like being thought of as a psychopath or a maniacal doll?"

"You bitch!" Chucky lifted his hand, which the male holding the female caught.

"You're wasting time." The male narrowed his dark eyes and shoved his target back a few steps. His fingers curled around the woman's throat. "Now, tell me what I want to know. Where...is...it?" he punctuated each word as his grip tightened.

"It's...gone," she choked out.

"Then you're of no use to me." In one swift move, he threw the chick they called Red off the dock and into the water. "Go back—"

A bullet struck the male in side of the head, cutting off his words. Before Gray lost his one chance, he aimed, pulled the trigger again, and shot his target. While he should take care of the other two, seconds counted with the woman. Maybe she'd get herself untied and back to the top, but he couldn't risk it. Gray tossed his rifle aside and raced down the tree.

Out of his periphery, he noted the two males sprawled on the pier, their blood pooling on the wooden planks. He'd address that once he got the female topside. The other two men had already run back toward the van. As much as he wanted to take care of it, the girl was more important right now. At least everything that happened wouldn't come back to his pod. No one would suspect him as a merman.

Popping the buttons on his shirt, he ripped it apart, threw it on the ground, and leaped over the railing. Gray dove into the cold, salty water with the finesse of a dancer. Although he didn't have his tail or fins at the moment, he could still swim. Thankfully, the current didn't work too much against him. His pants and shoes slowed him down a little.

At least they were near where the Atlantic Ocean and Hudson River met. He didn't know how fresh water affected his kind. It wasn't something he was prepared to discover. He swam through the blue water, using every muscle in his body to catch up to the sinking woman. As he got closer, he noticed she no longer struggled against her bindings. *Shit!* No way would she drown on his watch, which meant he only had one option to save her.

Though he loathed the idea of kissing her without permission, it was better than the alternative. Gray pushed harder and caught up to the female. Every second that passed brought her closer to death. Most mermaids or mermen used the kiss to delay the inevitable. It gave time for them to get a person to their leader. Except he wouldn't wish the pain of that transition on anyone.

This is the only choice, he told himself. He wrapped a hand around her slim waist, worked on one knot, and pressed his lips to hers, breathing air into her lungs. Though the kiss seemed to take his breath away, he'd do it again to save her life.

Lia stared wide-eyed at the male in front of her. What the fuck had he just done? How the hell was she breathing underwater? Better yet, what the fuck was he? Obviously, he was some kind of supernatural creature. Something to fret over later. The male got the last of her bindings undone. With no hesitation, she swam toward the surface, as did he. She didn't know what the fuck awaited her when she got to the top, but it was sure as shit better than what had just happened.

They broke the surface simultaneously. Lia eyed him as he ran a hand across the top of his head, slicking his dark hair back. Normally, she enjoyed taking in a chiseled body such as the specimen before her, except all she cared about was getting the fuck away from there. Her attention flicked to the pier. Without uttering a word, she swam toward it.

The male followed suit. Though his strokes were extremely more efficient than her own, he got to the dock just after she did. While she hadn't asked, he helped her climb onto the pier. Her gaze fell to the bodies splayed across the boardwalk. Droplets of blood and brain matter covered the ground. She glanced from the ashen color of Chucky's face to Sandor's...her eyes snapped back to the guy who'd saved her life. *Shit!* Had he done that? His lack of reaction suggested he had, which meant he didn't know.

Lia opened her mouth—the male grabbed Chucky's ankle and dragged him toward the pier's edge. The tatted, dark-haired male pointed at her. "Stay put. I'll be back in a minute." He dove off the pier, hauling Chucky's corpse into the water with him.

"Fuck that," she muttered and jumped to her feet. No way would she be here when Sandor fully healed and awoke. Shit. He'd snatched her phone from her. They'd nabbed her before she got her weapons. Maybe she couldn't properly kill him, but there might still be time for her to locate her phone. She couldn't have been in the water long. Right? Gripping a handful of wet hair, she wrung it out and groaned. Only one way to find out.

Reluctantly, Lia strode over to where Sandor's body lay. Her boots squeaked with each step she took. "Fuck," she mumbled as she kneeled beside the not-so-dead vampire. Quickly patting him down, Lia checked both pockets of his slacks and jacket. "Shit." Nothing. She scanned the wooden walkway and nearby parking lot. No van. Which meant the other two goons had run off. One of them probably had her cell phone.

Whatever. Hanging around waiting for that dumbass to return was a death sentence. Lia stood and started toward the city. She had to get back to her place before they found the hidden drive. If they found it first, then they would render all her efforts from the past five years useless. She couldn't let that happen. Even if it meant leaving the guy who'd saved her to face Sandor alone.

Lia ran across the walkway, stopped, water squishing into the grass beneath her wet boots, and glanced over her shoulder. Her rescuer could come back any second. It was insane to leave him to handle a vampire alone, especially if he didn't know shit about them. With how quickly they healed, Sandor would come around any second now. Except what would he worry over more? The guy who wasn't anywhere in sight or the thumb drive they'd tried to kill her to get? "Right."

Only one of those mattered more than the other. Without a second thought, Lia took off.

Chapter Two

Gray scowled as he stared at the dark-haired beauty standing in the window of a third-floor walkup. That little minx had gone against his order and left. That irritated the fuck out of him and left him with more than one question, which included what she'd done with the other body. When he'd returned to the surface after disposing of his target's corpse, the other one had disappeared, along with the female he'd rescued. There she stood, drying her hair as if she hadn't almost died.

None of that truly bothered him. No. His presence in front of her apartment building got to him. Why the fuck had he even come here? What was with this incessant need inside of him that demanded he find her? He dragged a hand across his face. "Fuck," he grumbled as he paced back and forth along the sidewalk. Gray glanced at the building across the street. If he had half a brain, he'd leave. He had no business getting involved with whatever shitstorm popped up in this woman's life. She wasn't his responsibility.

Out of his periphery, he noticed movement toward the building's entrance. Gray halted in his steps and narrowed his eyes at the shadowy figures. They looked familiar. *Shit!* Those were the two idiots who'd run off at the pier. They had to be there to finish the job or locate whatever they'd wanted from the woman. He gripped the back of his neck. An undying need to protect this female churned in the pit of his stomach. It didn't matter that he shouldn't intervene. Or that he'd completed his job and should return to his pod. No one expected him back for a few days.

"Fuck," he growled. Without another thought, he jogged across the street. They'd already slipped inside, but he had a damn good idea of where they headed. If only he knew the building better, he could cut them off, but too little too late. He'd simply have to wing it.

He grabbed the handle of the glass door, yanked it open, and headed inside. No buzzers or lock of any kind at the entrance. Even his building had some kind of security, and it was a shithole. The ding of the elevator drew his attention. It stopped at the third floor. Shit. Gray raced up the staircase, taking the steps two at a time.

Hitting the third-floor landing, he scanned the hallway in both directions. There were apartment doors to the left and right, but where had the men gone? He didn't see either of them. If nothing else, he expected to have heard some kind of commotion when they entered that woman's place. Given what he'd seen earlier, he stalked down to the left. Her apartment—a loud crash sounded on the other side of a door at the end of the hallway.

Gray darted toward the noise and kicked his booted foot into the door. It threw open, slamming into the wall. One male shook his head as he got to his feet, stepping on the glass shattered all around him, and lunged at the female. The other male faced Gray. Taking a couple of steps forward, Gray grabbed the guy by the throat. Blue jolts of lightning sparked across his skin as he electrified the male. The guy's body convulsed as the flesh beneath his palm reddened. Not that he released his hold. He wouldn't do that until the skin charred, and the room reeked of burned flesh.

His gaze flicked to his dark-haired beauty. Their eyes met briefly. She sidestepped her opponent's punch and countered with an uppercut to the jaw, forcing him to stumble backward. The corner of his mouth lifted. He may not know her name yet, but she was definitely worth the chase. A thick, putrid stench permeated the air. Gray glanced at the male in his grip. Recalling the electricity, he released his hold. The body crumpled to the floor. His grin widened at the sight of the male's blackened flesh.

He lifted his gaze—what the fuck? His eyes narrowed as his female elbowed the male he swore he'd killed at the pier. This couldn't be the same person. No one walked away from a headshot. Except, sure as fuck... The other man he'd found her fighting strode toward her. Gray reared back and launched himself at the male. Knocking the guy onto the wooden floor, he drove his fist into the male's chest. The male howled in pain. Lightning crackled across Gray's skin as he sent hundreds of volts of electricity coursing through the guy's body.

Keeping one eye on his victim, he peered at his female out of his periphery. She slammed the guy backward into the edge of the kitchen counter, twisted his arm, and flipped him over her shoulder. A glint of silver caught Gray's attention as the woman removed it from the back of her leather pants and struck her opponent in the chest, hitting the heart. Jumping to her feet, she took a couple of steps back and the male burst into flames.

What the fuck caught fire like that? He stared as a hot, red-orange blaze sizzled, consuming every bit of flesh without scorching the floor beneath the body. The embers had so much of his focus, he hardly noticed when the convulsing body beneath him charred. At least until the stench reached his nostrils. "Shit." Gray flicked his gaze to the remnants of the male he'd fought. The male's t-shirt had peeled away, looking like it had gotten caught in a fire with burned edges. Most of the male's chest had blackened. Smoke curled in the air as Gray recalled his power and rose to his feet, peering over his shoulder at the female.

Folding her arms across her chest, she glowered at him. "Did you fucking follow me?"

"Given that I've now saved you twice, that should be the least of your concerns," he retorted. Trouble obviously followed her wherever she went.

"Oh yeah, because you did that real well." She gestured to the two corpses on the ground and what remained of the third. Scoffing, she shook her head, stalked across the room, and shut the front door of the apartment. "Clearly, I had it under control."

Sure she had. Because if he hadn't intervened, she would've successfully taken them all out. Just like she'd done earlier. "Like you did at the dock? Or were you just practicing how long you could hold your breath underwater?"

"I would've been fine." She strode toward the hallway, the heels of her boots clicking with each step she took as she disappeared into the bedroom.

"Sure, Red." That was the name he'd heard the males call her. He couldn't exactly just holler 'hey, you' at her. "Keep telling yourself that. Maybe next time it'll be convincing." Gray followed her, lingering in the doorway of her bedroom. He cocked an eyebrow as she grabbed a few articles of clothing from a nearby dresser and shoved them into a duffle on the bed.

Her honey-brown eyes narrowed at him. "Lia. Only my friends call me Red."

He glanced over his shoulder at the two corpses. She couldn't mean they were her friends. His gaze flicked back in her direction. Lia darted to the dresser, collected a few more things, shoved them in the black duffle, and zipped it up. Then again, maybe she did. "Some friends," he muttered. "What are you doing?"

"What does it look like?" Lia ground her jaw and tossed the duffle over her shoulder. "Not only is The Grim Reaper sending people after me, but with all the noise we just made and my nosey neighbors, it's only a matter of minutes before the police show up. I plan to be gone before that happens." She stormed past him toward the living room.

The Grim Reaper? Something about that sounded familiar to him. Not that he could place it. Gray trailed behind her. He could fret over it later. Right now, he needed to get Lia some place safe. "Where do you plan to go?"

"Why does it fucking matter to you? Hell, I don't even know why I'm answering your questions. I don't fucking know you."

Grabbing her by the arm, he drew her back, almost flush against his body. A low rumble sounded in his chest. Fuck, she felt too damn good like this.

"Because I'm the one who's kept you alive. Seeing as you draw trouble to you like a fucking anglerfish, then I'd say I'm your best chance at staying that way."

Lia glared at him. "You mean like you disposed of the vampire? Oh, wait. That's right. *I* did that. Next time, try silver."

That certainly explained a few things. He knew the fuckers existed, though he'd never crossed paths with one. First time for everything. "And I handled all the rest. Now, what are you planning to do? Where are you planning to go?"

She yanked her arm from his hold. "If you must know, I'm going to finish what I started. While I don't need a babysitter, I also can't stop you from stalking me."

His eyebrows furrowed. Stalking? He hadn't stalked her. At least not in the complete sense of the word. Yes, he'd followed her, and he'd do it again if it's what it took to protect her. Gray scrubbed a hand across his face. Christ, this woman was going to kill him. "Be more specific," he growled. "What do you have that they wanted?"

Clenching her jaw, she folded her arms across her chest and glanced toward the bay window. "Information," Lia mumbled. "I have it all on a USB drive and a friend picked it up before those guys grabbed me. Now, I need to meet my friend at a club so I can finish what I started." She shoved a hand through her long, midnight black tresses. "You want to go with me, fine. I could use the ride, provided you have one. Though I would like to know who I'm traveling with."

Fuck, he wanted to fist a handful of her locks and bury his dick inside her. Where the hell had that come from? Releasing the sudden bout of desire that flooded him, he rolled his shoulders. "Gray. And I've got a ride."

"Good." Lia strutted to where the two bodies lay. She patted each one down. "Shit." Shaking her head, she stepped around the shattered coffee table and half-broken couch. "There's a fire escape just outside the kitchen window. We'll go out that way."

His gaze flicked toward the bay window. Police sirens wailed nearby. Gray held his hand out for her. "Come on. Let's go." They didn't have time to delay.

Lia stole another sidelong glimpse of Gray as she tapped her fingers against the table. She'd tried her damnedest not to notice his perfectly sculpted body as they'd ridden on his motorcycle to Club Athens. Now it was all she could see and recalled how taut it felt underneath her hands. Out of her periphery, she watched as his midnight blue eyes continuously scanned their surroundings. They sat in a booth at the back of the club. The same she would've chosen herself. It presented the best position to monitor everyone who came and went. Not that she saw anyone but him, even as they waited for their waitress to retrieve her contact, the club owner.

Gray stretched his long, muscular legs out and readjusted in the booth for the third time. He ran a hand through his dark tousled hair as he scoured the crowd gathered at the bar and eyed the group at the club's entrance. His black t-shirt stretched with each movement. Not that it covered everything. A couple of tattoos on each of his biceps played peekaboo. The ones that really stood out were the ace of clubs on his left forearm and the crisscrossed daggers on his right. In the mafia, both signified him as an assassin, but they had to mean something else. She knew all those who worked for the boss, including the supernaturals.

Gods, she needed to stop staring. It didn't matter if every inch of him was lickable. She had a job to do. Nothing else mattered. Especially not some stranger who'd forced himself into her life. Lia surveyed the room as more customers filled various parts of the bar and took up seats at the oak tables. She watched as patrons passed the shimmering dark green walls. No matter which way she looked, this club always reminded her of a forest.

"How long are we going to wait?" Gray asked.

"However long it takes." Not like they had any other choice. Otis had the drive she needed. She couldn't do shit without it. Lia picked up her glass bottle and took a swig of beer. She should be used to this by now. How many times had she done this dance with Otis? The male made her wait any chance he got. It annoyed the fuck out of her. At least it gave her the opportunity to clock his guards and any other supernaturals among the partygoers.

Although the bouncers at the entrance were human, the other four that stood around the building were vampires. One by the bar, another by the kitchen doorway, and the other two near the back hallway. Those didn't include the two she spotted at a table on the first level. At least none of them looked familiar. One less thing to worry about. Lia sipped her beer. Her eyes settled on Otis as he approached the table. *About fucking time.*

"I apologize for making you wait." He swept his long blond hair over his shoulder, his amber eyes narrowing at Lia. "Though I have told you before that we don't conduct business here."

"Not really a choice this time." It wasn't a rule that had ever changed. She'd almost always complied with it. Almost. They'd only had this conversation once or twice in the past.

"Of course," Otis replied. He flicked his gaze at Gray. "Your companion will have to leave."

Gray sat up straighter. His midnight blue eyes darkened. "I'm not going anywhere. So, I suggest you sit, so we can get this handled."

"It's fine, Otis." Besides, Gray had her back. Even if he couldn't kill a vampire, she could. Not that she planned for them to fight their way out, but better to be prepared.

Otis leaned forward, placing his hands on the cherry oak table, and got close to her. "You and I have an agreement, Red. We don't have discussions in my place of business, nor do we conduct them around strangers."

She quickly tired of his attitude and all the pushback. It had already taken far longer than she expected. What option did she have? She could play hardball, but all she had to threaten him with was the silver blade tucked into her boot.

A slight click sounded over the din. Gray glowered at Otis. "I recently discovered what silver does to your kind. I'm *dying* to try it out. Keep being difficult and you'll burn before your guards reach their weapons. Or avoid the pain and answer her questions. Understood?"

Hot damn. Didn't that just make her so-called rescuer sexier? Lia eyed her friend's bodyguards. If any of them heard the noise, none of them reacted. She'd had a shitty day. If this was what it took to make it better, so be it.

Clenching his jaw, Otis carefully slid into the booth next to her. "What do you want?"

The corner of her mouth upturned. Good. Now, they could get this done and over with so she could move on to the next part of her plan. "The item you retrieved from my apartment earlier."

"I don't have it."

"Excuse me?" Lia shook her head. No, that wasn't right. She'd seen the brick removed in the wall when she'd gotten home. Anytime she ever needed him to retrieve something, that's where she placed it. They were the only ones who knew about it. How the fuck did he not have it? "You told me you'd get it and it wasn't in our hiding place."

"It was daytime, Red. The sun really isn't my friend. So…I sent…an advocate in my stead."

A low rumble sounded in Gray's chest. "What the fuck does that mean?"

Fuck. If she hadn't wanted to stab him before, she sure as shit did now. "That he sent one of his blood bags."

"You know how much I despise that term."

"Fine. How about blood whore? Is that better?" Because either way, it was the same damn thing. Shit. This certainly presented a problem. She had to think of a way to fix it. Nothing could happen without that damn drive.

"No." Otis draped one leg over the other and clasped his hands in his lap. "Though I suppose it concludes our business, does it not?"

"The fuck it does." Their business wasn't finished until she had what she needed. Lia smirked. "I'm gonna make this real easy. Call the blood bag you sent and either get them here or find out what they did with my property. Because if you don't, I'm gonna make sure Tatya learns all about the competition. How do you think that would make your wife feel? Like just another conquest or someone else for you to use."

With an exasperated sigh, Otis dug his cell phone out of the inside pocket of his Armani jacket. "You really used to be much more fun, Red." He glanced at Gray as he pulled up his contacts. "Has she told you how she earned the nickname 'Red'?"

"It's not important," Gray replied. "Now, how about you make your fingers do some talking and stop wasting our damn time?"

"You really can pick them, Red." Hovering his finger over his cell phone, Otis selected a contact and pressed the phone to his ear. It rang twice before a feminine voice came on the line. "Hello, darling. Did you get that item we spoke of earlier?"

"Yes, though I'm guessing you're not the one asking," the woman stated.

A shiver shot down Lia's spine as she listened to the phone conversation. Who the fuck was this chick? Something about the female's voice sounded familiar, though she couldn't place it. Even if she could, how could they know Otis hadn't questioned the whereabouts of the drive?

"That is an accurate assessment."

"Let me speak to her."

"As you wish." Otis held the cell phone out to Lia. "For you, my dear."

Lia raised an eyebrow at him. Who the fuck wanted to talk to her? How'd they even know who she was, or that she'd asked about the drive? Fuck. Only one way to find out. Accepting the cell phone, Lia pressed it to her ear. "Hello?"

"Here I thought you'd run away. It is your motto."

Her eyes shut briefly as her sister's voice came across the line. This wasn't happening. She hadn't spoken to her family members in over ten years. Not since the day they kicked her out of the house. A day she'd never forget.

"Get out!" her father screamed.

"Daddy, please!" Lia pleaded. What could she do to make her family understand? Why couldn't they see things from her perspective?

"No! No daughter of mine is this tenderhearted. We kill supernatural creatures. Not let them continue to roam this earth so they can destroy everything beautiful about this world."

"But they're not all bad. Some of them go out of their way—"

"To torture humans. That's what they all do. I'll hear no more excuses from you, Natalia. From this day forth, we'll no longer recognize you as family. Now, get out of my sight before disowning you is the least of your problems."

One by one, each of her family members turned their backs on her. Tears welled in the corners of her eyes as she walked away from the only life she'd ever known. She'd just have to forge her own path now.

For a split second, she considered correcting her sister. Except that wouldn't get them anywhere. Especially if Otis had sent the female to retrieve the drive. "What do you want, Nina?"

Gray's eyebrows furrowed, though she didn't dare answer the unspoken question.

"An exchange."

"Name your terms and we'll talk."

"It's simple, really. You give me a hundred thousand dollars and I'll give you the drive."

Lia smirked. "You want money?" Why ask for something so menial? It didn't make a bit of sense. Her sister wasn't exactly materialistic. Their parents hadn't raised them that way. Most hunters weren't. Although she hadn't seen the female in ten years. Maybe something had changed during that time. Which seemed accurate if the female allowed a vampire to feed on her. No hunter had ever done that.

"Assuming you don't want The Grim Reaper to get a hold of this, yes. Of course, if you're good with him having it, I'll be happy to pass it along."

Shit. She'd encrypted the damn thing. The only way her sister knew about him...was if she'd cracked it. Lia glanced at Gray. She didn't have that kind of money on hand. Maybe with his help, that wouldn't matter. "It'll take me a bit to get it together. I'll text you a time and place to meet tomorrow."

"You have twenty-four hours, sis. After that...this will go to the highest bidder."

The phone line went dead. Lia ground her jaw. "You should really be more careful about who you feed from."

"I'll take that into consideration." Otis flashed a pearly grin and slipped out of the booth.

Narrowing her eyes, Lia held the phone out to the male. "On second thought." She tucked it into her leather halter. "This is my fee for the stunt you pulled." If he'd retrieved the drive himself, none of this would've happened.

"Fine. Then consider our arrangement terminated." He flicked his amber eyes to her companion. "For the record, we call her Red because of all the red flags. She's a walking bomb ready to go off at any second."

Gray shifted in the booth. "Good thing I'm not afraid of an explosion." He climbed out and held out his hand to Lia.

Sliding out after him, she clasped his hand. Fuck, she needed one hell of a plan. One that fixed everything because there was no way her sister cared about the money, which meant this was a set up. But for what?

Chapter Three

G ray opened the door to his loft-style apartment. He stepped aside, giving Lia berth to waltz by him. His place wasn't much, but he'd selected it that way on purpose. This allowed him to conduct his work without drawing unnecessary attention. Plus, people didn't think he had anything worth stealing. The number of things of value he kept in his home would astonish people, especially his pod.

"What are we doing here?" Lia peered over her shoulder at him.

"It's someplace safe where we can crash for the night." He shut the front door and flipped three deadbolts, locking them in together. No one knew about his apartment. It had taken him years to procure the right location. Even longer to make it something habitable, where he could hide all the tools of his trade.

"Crash? As in...you expect me to sleep here? You're fucking insane!" She stormed toward the door, her bag bouncing against her hip with each step. "No. Just take me to a motel."

Gray stepped in front of her, blocking her exit. "And what? Hope for the best? I don't think so. If I have to save you again, I'd rather it be on my turf. Now, turn around. You can have the bed."

"Excuse me? Save me? Again? What?" She glared at him. "You think telling one stupid vampire that you've got silver bullets makes you my savior? Because if memory serves, you didn't kill the first one. I did. Without *your* help. I didn't need it then and sure as fuck don't need it now."

"Like you didn't with the humans or at the dock. Right. I forgot. Your lungs weren't burning with agonizing restraint, clinging to every breath as you struggled against your bindings." He took a step closer, daring her to argue with him. While he shouldn't, he just couldn't help himself. There was something about her that drew him to her. "Just like you didn't fight against every drop of water that you slipped through, continuously pulling you down farther into its murky depths."

Lia clenched her jaw. "Fine. Don't take me. Just move out of my way and I'll walk to one myself."

Fuck, she looked sexy as hell, staring at him like that with one hip popped out. He wanted to kiss her again with more desperation than he'd ever felt in his life. Not that it would do a damn thing to get through to her. There was only one way to accomplish that. Gray stepped aside and gestured toward the door.

She strode forward a couple of steps.

He grabbed her by the arm, spun her around, and shoved her against the door. Stepping in close, he pinned her in so she couldn't escape. She'd have no choice but to listen now. "You can deny the truth all you want, but it won't change it. Maybe things were under control in your apartment. None of that would've been possible if I hadn't intervened at the docks. I jumped into the Hudson and pulled you out. Now, I don't know what kind of trouble is lurking around the corner, but it would be wise that you accept the facts and help I've offered. I won't do it again." He'd uttered nothing except the truth until that last line. Whether she accepted it or not, he'd watch her. He couldn't let her go.

Drawing herself up to her full height, nearly six feet with the four-inch stiletto boots she had on, she thrust her chin and jutted out her chest. Lia closed the distance between them, getting into his personal space. "Why? You looking for some kind of *thank you*? Or a reward?" She laid her hands on his chest and slowly dragged her fingers down his six-pack. Heat flushed her cheeks and neck. "Or maybe...you're just trying to get another taste?"

Oh, he wanted to taste more than that defiant mouth of hers. The desire to stroke every part of her body with his tongue and slam his cock deep into that pussy of hers set his veins on fire. Especially with how she touched him right then. Fuck, not once over the last twenty years had he found himself *this* attracted to someone. Hell, longer than that. If he gave it too much thought...a low rumble sounded in his chest. "I want it all, sweetheart." He claimed her lips, driving his tongue into her mouth.

Lia moaned as she deepened the kiss, dropped the bag from her shoulder, and stepped into his body.

Wrapping a hand around her waist, he tugged her flush against him. Her firm tits hit his chest. Gray groaned. Fuck, she felt damn good. Better than anything he'd held in years. He desired more of her in his grip and on his tongue. The slight battle between them wasn't enough. Her fingers trailed a path over his pectoral muscles. She grabbed onto his shoulders, giving him all the encouragement he needed.

Gray slid his hands down her body, gripped her ass, and lifted her off the floor. Without hesitation, her legs came around his waist. He growled into the kiss as he tightened the hold he had on her with one hand and fisted a handful of her soft locks with the other. His cock thickened in his pants, throbbing with an urgency he'd never known before. Not that he minded in the least.

Grinding against his shaft, Lia dragged her nails down his back. She curled her fingers around the bottom of his t-shirt and yanked it out of his pants. The kiss broke off as she swept it over his head and tossed it aside. Through their ragged breaths, their gazes locked.

Her eyelids hooded over her honey-brown eyes as she bit her bottom lip. *Fuck.* That look was enough to make him come right where he stood. She wanted him as much as he wanted her. Lia fused their lips together, entangling their tongues in an epic battle. One he had no problem entering.

As Lia ran her hands across his biceps, he worked at the knot where her halter tied around the back of her neck. It took every ounce of willpower not to tear the damn thing, especially as she rocked her hips and generated more friction between them. Getting the knot undone, he pressed her back against the door and yanked her top down. Covering her tit with his palm, Gray massaged her breast. Her nipple pebbled beneath his hand. He groaned at the feel of her silky flesh.

Fuck! She tasted better than any sweet that had ever hit his tongue. This was nowhere near enough. Breaking off the kiss, he dropped his head, sucked her breast into his mouth, and stroked his tongue across her nipple.

"Oh, gods!" she moaned. Her back arched, pushing her tit more into his mouth.

His cock strained against his pants. The leather stretched a little. It practically pinched his shaft, heightening the ache in his balls. Fuck, he couldn't wait to get inside her. No time for the bedroom. He needed her too badly. Gray removed the last of her leather halter and threw it over his shoulder, where it landed somewhere on the floor. Although he'd handled it with care, he couldn't do the same with her pants.

In a comingled mess of hands, they worked on the buttons of each other's bottoms. It didn't take long at all for Lia to free his dick from his leathers. No more time than it took him to tug her pants down to her knees. She unhooked her ankles from his back. He shifted his hold and pinned her thighs against her abdomen. Gray angled the head of his cock to her entrance and slammed deep inside of her pussy in one stroke. They both cried out in ecstasy.

Gray pulled his hips back and drove his dick back inside of her. "Fuck," he grunted. Although she was wet, she was also tight. She fit him like a second skin. Every stroke sent a jolt of lightning across his synapses. It was almost like touching a live wire. One that felt like pure heaven.

Lia dug her nails into his back. "Fuck, don't stop."

"Not stopping." Not unless she told him to do so. As he pistoned in and out of her, increasing his pace, he fused their lips together. Their tongues swirled together in an exquisite dance. One of her hands slapped against the door as she rocked her hips, meeting each one of his thrusts.

Holy shit. He was already on the verge of an orgasm. How was that even remotely possible? Even with this uncontrollable need he had for her, he'd never once come so soon. Nothing about this night made a lick of sense to him. Gripping her ass tighter, Gray pounded into her. Not that it impacted her movements at all. Lia kept a perfect pace with him.

Her nails raked his shoulder. She nipped his tongue, threw her head back, and cried out, "Fuck!" as the walls of her pussy clenched around his shaft.

Just as she came, squirting all over his cock, his balls tightened, and his orgasm detonated inside of him. It shot up the length of his dick, exploding out of him. "Fuck!" Gray barked. He drilled into her, carrying them both through their releases. His hips didn't stop until their mutual climaxes ended.

Panting, Gray dropped his head into the crook of her neck. Holy shit. Although his hips stilled, his cock twitched inside of her. Despite how perfect that was, he was far from through. Maybe he didn't understand how all of this happened, but he didn't give a shit right now. That was tomorrow's problem.

"That was amazing," Lia cooed.

Gray swept his tongue along her throat. Fuck, she tasted like sweet water and he had to have more. With a low growl, he brushed a kiss across her shoulder, slipped his erection from the warmth of her pussy, and adjusted the hold he had on her ass. "You haven't seen anything yet."

This time, he'd strip her of all her clothes. That way, he could devour her properly and give her a night neither of them would ever forget.

Lia cracked one eye open as light streamed in through the window. Fuck. What the hell came over her last night? Not that she'd complain too much. She hadn't gotten with anyone in a long time. Although she was gloriously sore, last night was a onetime thing. With a satisfied groan, she rolled over onto her back and stretched her arms above her head. The bed was empty.

Small miracle.

She'd expected to find Gray in bed beside her. The sound of the shower coming on hit her ears. Explained where he'd gone. Clutching the sheet to her breasts, Lia sat up and surveyed the apartment. She hadn't inspected it as she normally would. Well, now seemed like a good time to snoop, especially with him in the shower. Where had her clothes ended up? Shit, she didn't know. Fuck it. Tossing the covers aside, Lia climbed out of bed. Though she quickly located her pants on the floor, nothing else was in the bedroom.

She couldn't exactly stand there naked. Her gaze landed on a black t-shirt laid across the top of the dresser. It would work. Lia picked it up and tugged it over her head. It hit the tops of her thighs and smelled highly masculine and woodsy. Her belly fluttered as a shiver shot down her spine. What the hell was that? She wasn't a weak-in-the-knees kind of girl. That reaction had certainly come out of nowhere. Shaking the sensations off, she focused her attention on the room.

As much as she wanted to check out the books on his bookcase, comb through the drawers of his nightstands and dresser, and scour through the rest of his things, she needed to find her bag first. Where had she left it? Right. She'd dropped it by the door last night before they fucked. How could it have slipped her mind?

Tiptoeing across the hardwood floor, she descended the two steps into the front half of his apartment and crossed over to the front door. He had a strange setup in his place. No bedroom door existed. The kitchen stood to her right, with the living room directly in front of that. Although he had sparse furniture and no real décor that she noticed, it was completely spacious. It didn't look like any bachelor pad she'd ever seen. What was he hiding?

Lia collected her bag and top from the floor and surveyed the apartment once again. Her gaze flicked briefly to the bathroom. If she planned to snoop, now was the time. She might have a few more minutes at best before he exited the bathroom. Determined to learn something about her rescuer, she returned to the bedroom and tossed her bag and halter onto the bed.

Crouching on her haunches, she scanned the book titles on the bottom and top shelves of the bookcase. It comprised a multitude of non-fiction books, including a few on New York City's geography. Boring as fuck. Rising to her full height of five-feet-eight inches, she opened the two small drawers in the nightstand. Neither contained anything of interest. Thus far, nothing she'd seen told her a damn thing about this guy.

Her gaze narrowed as she stared at the wall. There was something off about it. Lia leaned in closer. Was that a divot? She ran her fingers across the small space in the wood. No. It had a crevice. It was...a button. Without a second thought, she depressed the button. A compartment to the left of it flipped open.

"Holy shit," Lia muttered as she drank in the four guns and two daggers stored inside the secret chamber. Her gaze flicked between the two 22s, 9MM, and the 38. Although she'd noticed the six-inch steel blades, her attention remained focused on the 9MM Sig. As much as she liked a good revolver, she preferred a semi-automatic. Something she didn't currently have in her possession.

She stole a sidelong glance at the bathroom door. The shower hadn't shut off yet, but she expected it would anytime now. Biting the inside of her cheek, Lia eyed the Sig Sauer again. She picked it up in her hand, curled her fingers around the grip, and held it for a moment. It hardly weighed a thing.

The water's spray shut off, trickling into nothing more than a drizzle. Lia pressed the button. The compartment closed just as silently as it had opened. She unzipped her bag, buried the gun under her clothes, and shut it. A second later, the bathroom door opened.

Gray stood in the doorway with his wet, tousled hair swept to the side. Droplets of water sluiced down his six-pack, stopping just at the top of the towel wound tightly around his waist. *Fuck.* He looked so damn delectable. She bit her bottom lip. Okay, she seriously shouldn't want to ride him again or run her fingers over every tattoo. Especially since other things took priority. Lia gripped her shoulder. "Are you done?"

"Uh, yeah." He strode out into the bedroom and walked around the bed toward the dresser. Stopping, his gaze flicked to her. "Are you wearing my shirt?"

"It was accessible," she retorted as she passed by him and headed to the bathroom. It was the only way she could stop staring at him.

"Come into the kitchen when you're finished. We need to discuss the meeting you set."

Yeah, they definitely had to do that. As much as she wished they didn't, she had to plan for all possibilities regarding her sister. And she couldn't handle this alone. Lia paused in the doorway to the bathroom just as he dropped the towel, giving her a great shot of his perfectly round ass. She barely squashed the purr in her chest. Fuck. He really needed to stop this. Gripping the doorframe, she swallowed the lump in her throat. "Yeah. We'll do that."

"Good."

Like she had any other choice. Lia disappeared into the bathroom, shutting the door behind her. Another room that didn't have any kind of décor. No cute little sayings or anything like it. Nothing outside the normal shower curtain. Even that was simple. Who the hell had she slept with? Aside from a guy who collected weapons. She didn't know if that should unnerve her or make her feel protected.

Not that it mattered. She didn't have anyone else to turn to for help. Lia blew out a heavy breath and ran a hand across the top of her head. She strode over to the toilet, lifted the lid, and sat down. "Fuck me." Nothing about this was ideal. Depending on some guy she'd just met, no knowledge of his species or capabilities, and the crap with her sister.

Why would Nina have asked for money? It didn't make a damn bit of sense. Hunters required little in the way of funds. Most of everything they made themselves. Guns were the only exception, but not all hunters used them. As of ten years ago, that included her family. Had something changed? Lia finished her business, cleaned up, stood, and flushed the toilet. As she washed her hands, she stared at her reflection as if it would answer her questions.

She rolled her neck, shut the water off, and dried her hands on the blue towel hanging on the rack. Although she hadn't figured it all out, only one thing made sense regarding her family. Fuck, she really hoped that wasn't the case. Lia opened the bathroom door and the smoky aroma of bacon wafted into the room. Her stomach rumbled. Damn, that smelled like heaven.

"I hope you're hungry," Gray called out.

"Sure am," she replied as she made her way to the kitchen. "I worked up one hell of an appetite last night."

A smirk crossed his face as he stacked a few strips of bacon on a plate. "Talk to me about that conversation you had. Who'd you talk to?"

"It was my sister." They had discussed none of it last night. Instead, they'd gotten physical. Man, watching him work on breakfast turned her on all over again. How could she want someone so badly? Fuck, she needed to gain control of her body. The damn hussy.

He glanced over his shoulder as he placed three more strips in the frying pan. "Your sister?"

"Yes. She wants money." Rolling her shoulders, Lia strode farther into the kitchen and hopped up on the marble counter. "Not that I know where she'd think I'd have what she's asking for, except…"

"What?"

"It's not her style. I feel like I'm missing something, but I can't figure out what."

"Well, you said you'd pick the time and place, so we'll use that to our advantage."

Lia cocked an eyebrow at him. "Our?" He inserted himself before she even had the chance to ask for his assistance. Well, that took care of that problem.

He flipped the sizzling bacon, picked up one of the cooked pieces, and bit into it as he faced her. "We covered this last night. I'm not letting you out of my sight."

Right. How could she have forgotten? Of all the things he'd pointed out multiple times, that had been among them. "Fine." Lia let out an exasperated sigh. It was better this way, but she didn't have to make it easy on him. "She gave me twenty-four hours at most. I'd prefer to do it all in daylight. There's a warehouse we can use. Should give us excellent positions all around."

Gray finished things up, removed the pan from the burner, and shut it off. He placed the bacon strips onto the plate as his eyebrows furrowed. Leaning against the counter, he folded his arms across his chest. "Do you always plan for every probability?"

"It's better than ending up dead because you overlooked something simple." It was the long answer, but so what? She covered her ass however she could.

"We'll need some help." His gaze traveled her body, and his tongue snaked out across his bottom lip.

Heat shot straight to her core. Fuck. He needed to stop looking at her like that, otherwise they'd never eat. Although they had time to eat and fuck, but shouldn't food come first? "Definitely. Know anyone with some skill?"

He pushed off the counter, closed the distance between them, and set a hand on either side of her hips. "Something like that." Gripping the hem of the t-shirt in his palms, he slid it up a little farther. "We've got time to get all of that figured out. Right now, something else is calling my attention."

"Care to share?" Though she had a damn good idea. It was the same thing she wanted. Lia scooted forward a little and wrapped her legs around his waist. She ran her fingers over the tattoo of a blade stabbed through a skull on his left biceps.

"Seems like you already know." He fused their lips together in a deep kiss.

Entangling her tongue with his, she deepened the kiss. Fuck, he tasted good. Almost like the most intoxicating honey she'd ever sampled. She could so easily get drunk off of him. Trailing her fingers over his shoulders, she raked her nails down his back and made a mental note of every bunched muscle beneath her hand. He had a body she could play on for days and still never get enough.

He growled into the kiss, sending shivers down her spine. As Gray grabbed her ass with one hand, his fingers traced slow circles along her inner thigh and inched closer to her slit with each maneuver.

Fuck. His touch headed exactly where she wanted. Her legs loosened of their own volition, spreading her thighs wider and giving him more room to work. Though it wasn't the only thing she desired. As much as she longed for him to touch her, she needed to touch him. Lia slipped her fingertips inside the waistband of his sweats and lazily ran them back and forth across his soft flesh.

Dipping his fingers in the folds of her pussy, he stroked her clit and lit up every synapse in her body. Lia groaned. *Fuck, yes.* As amazing as it felt, she had this uncontrollable need for more. She rocked her hips against his hand. In a single move, Gray drove two of his fingers inside her pussy. He pistoned them in and out as he rubbed her clit with his thumb.

Holy shit. It was like he'd read her mind.

Gray fisted a handful of her hair, yanked her head back, and skimmed his lips along her neck. "You like that? The way I touch this sweet pussy of yours?"

"Yes," she groaned. "Don't stop."

"Definitely not doing that." Emphasizing his words, he inserted a third finger and thrusted them in and out faster.

"Harder," Lia demanded. The inner walls of her pussy clenched around his fingers, intensifying the heat coursing through her body. Fuck. At this rate, it wouldn't take her long to come. Not that it was enough. She shoved her hand in his pants, curled her fingers around his thick shaft, and stroked up and down his rigid length.

"You forgot to say *please*, pet." He nipped at her earlobe and tugged on her hair. "Say it and I'll give you what we both know you *really* want."

Not once had she ever begged for anything regarding sex. Except he was right. His fingers weren't what she actually desired. She yearned for something akin to a repeat of last night. If she had to utter a single word, a small plea to get what they both wanted, fuck, she'd do it without hesitation. "Harder...please," Lia pleaded.

"Good girl." Gray removed his digits from her pussy, sucked her juices from them, and grabbed the hem of the t-shirt she wore. In one move, he forced her hand from his pants, swept the shirt over her head, and tossed it aside. Gripping the back of her neck, he lashed his tongue across her nipple and slowly lowered her down against the cool marble counter.

Curling his fingers around her thighs, he trailed kisses down her body and swept his tongue along the slit of her pussy. With a slight whimper, she grabbed the edge of the countertop above her head. Fuck, yes. That was exactly where she needed him, though it still wasn't enough.

"Do you want more, pet?" He blew air across her folds and brushed a soft kiss across her inner thigh. "Tell me what you want, pet. I need to hear it."

Shivers shot down her spine. Holy shit. No one had ever said anything like that to her before. It wasn't just the command of his words, but the guttural sound of his voice. "Your tongue," she rasped. "Fuck me with your tongue...please."

"That's my good girl." Gray fused his mouth to her pussy and drove his tongue deep inside of her. He didn't waste a second building up a steady pace. Instead, he swirled his tongue and fucked her with it hard and fast.

"Fuck!" Lia screamed as her back arched and her hips rocked against his tongue. A bolt of lightning speared across every nerve-ending in her body. Her thighs tensed as his fingers dug into her flesh. "Harder, please," she begged.

Gray complied with her request. He thrusted his tongue in and out of her harder and faster and tightened the grip he had on her thighs. The slight sting intensified the heat that raged in her core. She cried out in pure ecstasy. Her pussy clenched as an orgasm ripped through her body and exploded into his mouth. He didn't stop going at her until he'd swallowed every drop of her cum.

Straightening up, Gray swept his forefinger and thumb along the outside of his mouth and the small patch of hair on his chin. As he stared at her through hooded eyes, he cleaned the remnants of her orgasm from his hand. "Don't move," he growled.

Oh, she had no intention of doing that. Especially not with the way he looked at her right then. Her tongue snaked out across her lower lip as he hooked his thumbs in the waistband of his sweats and took them off. Before she could utter a word, he slammed his cock deep inside of her, all the way to the hilt. "Oh, god," she moaned.

Clutching her thighs, his fingers curled around her flesh hard enough to leave marks. He pounded in and out of her, stretching her beyond her limit. "Fuck," Gray grunted.

Fuck was right. Each stroke of his thick shaft sent a jolt of lightning across her synapses, stoking the blaze burning hot in her body. Intense pleasure scorched her nerve-endings. She gripped the edge of the countertop so tightly sweat beaded along her palm. Unable to help herself, Lia dug the heels of her feet into his ass and lifted her hips, meeting each of his thrusts.

As he increased his pace, he covered one of her breasts with his hand and rolled her nipple between his thumb and forefinger.

"Harder...please," she whimpered. Each new touch took her higher and higher. Almost to the point it felt like she soared. Gray had become this fantastic drug she couldn't get enough of. No matter how much of him she had, she still needed more. And he seemed all too happy to give her another hit.

Skimming his fingertips across her skin, he gripped her back and sat her up as she released the hold she had on the counter. His lips crashed against hers and their tongues entangled in a deep kiss. Tugging her body flush against his, he fisted a handful of her hair and drilled into her. The new angle allowed his cock to penetrate deeper. Her feet pressed harder against his ass as her thighs tensed and the volcano that burned hot inside of the two of them erupted.

Together, they both cried out in ecstasy. Holding on tight to one another, neither of them stilled until they'd worked through their mutual orgasm. Their gazes met. Something sparkled in those midnight blue orbs of his. Not that she could say what, just that her stomach flip-flopped. She had to look away before anything else fluttered inside of her body. Lia focused on the sheen of sweat covering his chest. The corner of her mouth lifted. "Looks like you need another shower," she said, breaking the silence.

"I'd say so, but..." his words trailed off as he skimmed his lips over her throat and ear. "Who said I'm done with you?" His cock twitched, still buried inside of her.

A shiver shot down her spine. Fuck. She didn't know how this man had so much stamina, yet she fucking loved it. "We can always kill two birds and conserve some water."

"Mmm, I like the way you think." Getting a good grip on her ass, he lifted her off the counter and carried her toward the bathroom.

"Me, too," she purred. "Me, too." Because regardless of what transpired later today, at least she had fun getting there.

Chapter Four

Gray pulled into a parking spot. His gaze flicked toward the row of motorcycles to his left, landing on one with a lightning bolt across the fuel tank. Perfect. The one he needed was there. Not that he hadn't expected otherwise, but at least now he knew for sure. He shut off the ignition, dropped the kickstand, and ensured it supported the weight of his motorcycle before he removed his helmet.

"Please tell me you're joking," Lia said as she slipped her hands from around his waist.

"About?"

"You didn't just seriously bring me to the Moonlit Devils Motorcycle Club, home to a shifter pack."

Glancing over his shoulder, he cocked an eyebrow at her. "How do you know that?" He hadn't uttered a word about his friend. Or that the one person in the city he trusted was a shifter. Although maybe it shouldn't surprise him. She'd already crossed paths with multiple vampires. Did that mean...was she a supernatural creature? Something he'd just overlooked? The angel wings tattoo she had on her lower back hadn't indicated anything of the sort.

Taking the helmet off, she rested it on her thigh and leaned in closer. "I'm a fucking hunter. It's my job to know these places. You're insane if you think I'll be safe here."

"A hunter?" he muttered. Shit. How had he not noticed that? She moved faster and carried more strength than any human he'd seen before. Yeah, she'd kicked that vampire's ass, but it hadn't even occurred to him Lia was anything out of the ordinary. Though they couldn't alter the course now. Even if they could, he didn't have anyone else to turn to for help. At least not on land. Or in the city.

"Yes, and just because I'm different and I've worked with supernaturals in the past doesn't mean they'll be happy to see me."

"You're with me, so you'll be fine." Besides, the alpha owed him big. Gray hung his helmet on the handlebars. "Now let's go. We're burning daylight."

Throwing her hands up in defeat, Lia dismounted the motorcycle. "Fine, but if we end up in a fight, you're getting the worst fucking *I told you so* ever."

He cocked an eyebrow at her. "Are you always this cynical?" Even in his line of work, he didn't expect the worst. That was saying something.

Glowering at him, she folded her arms across her chest. "I'm a realist and people rarely disappoint."

With a shake of his head, he climbed off the Harley, took her helmet from her hands, and set it on the bike. "People might surprise you." It had happened more than once since he'd turned. Flashing a toothy grin, he draped an arm across her shoulders. "All you have to do is act like my old lady."

"So, I should stare at you with indignation, like I'm secretly plotting how to kill you? Or do you expect me to fawn over you like a school girl?"

The corner of his mouth lifted into a crooked smile. "Somewhere in between." He liked that smart mouth of hers, for her to be anything other than true to herself. The pack needed to buy exactly what he sold. That her life mattered to him, which wasn't entirely a lie. Yeah, he'd only known her for a day, but he'd do whatever it took to protect her. Even if it meant cashing in a favor.

"Oh, so like I both love and hate you and the emotion I'm feeling just depends on the day of the week."

"Something like that," he conceded, as they headed around the corner toward the entrance. Fuck, she needed to stop getting so damn sarcastic. Because if she kept it up, he'd show her exactly how much it affected him. Although maybe if he did, she'd get the picture.

"Okay, then today," she started as she slipped from under his arm, "is a day that I'm pissed at you."

A low rumble resounded in his chest. He whipped around and pinned her against the outer wall, pressing his body flush to hers. "I said I'd protect you and that's what I'm going to do, especially as you have a habit of bringing chaos into your life. Now, as much as I enjoy that mouth of yours, you need to stop fucking around. You know just what you need to do."

Her honey-brown eyes narrowed at him. "I will when you acknowledge the fucking fact that you're taking me into a dangerous situation."

"I'm well aware of how it appears. How about you trust that despite that, I know what I'm doing?" Because he did. Mostly. The only thing he couldn't quite explain was her and this deep-rooted need to protect her. Regardless of what he had to sacrifice.

"Except I don't know a damn thing about you."

Gray leaned in close and whispered in her ear, "You knew me pretty damn well this morning, pet." Something he hadn't forgotten a second of and planned to repeat before the sea called him home.

"Just because we fucked doesn't mean I know shit about you. You want me to trust you, then tell me something real." Lia smirked. "Or are you incapable of that?"

He opened his mouth and snapped it shut. Shit. While he hated to admit it, she had a point. They had shared little of anything with one another. That wasn't entirely true. He'd kept his life a secret, yet insisted on learning things about her. Gray let out an exasperated sigh and ran a hand through his hair. "I can't give you details, but I can tell you this. The alpha owes me...for saving his life. That's why I'm confident you'll be safe as long as you're with me."

"Oh." Mischief sparkled in her eyes. She patted his cheek. "Now, was that so hard?"

Did she just play him? To get information? If the shit-eating grin on her face was anything to go by, he'd say yes. Well, hell. He might've deserved that. Gray closed the distance between them and pressed his lips to hers, entangling her tongue in a deep kiss. Fuck, she tasted too damn good. As much as he wanted to teach her a lesson, now wasn't the time. He broke off the kiss and nipped at her. "Not at all. Now be a good girl, just like you were this morning, pet."

"Oh, I'll be good," she purred. "I promise." Lia ducked under his arm, slipping away from him, and sashayed toward the door.

Fuck. The way she swung her hips...he barely bit back a growl. Pure torture. Two could play at that.

She paused and glimpsed over her shoulder at him. "Coming?"

With two long strides, Gray caught up to her. He draped an arm across her shoulder, tugged her close, and brushed a kiss across the side of her neck. "Later. Much later. Right now, we've got business to attend."

Lia scanned the room as they entered the bar. All conversation ceased and everyone jerked their heads toward them. She tightened the grip she had on Gray's waist. God, this was such a bad idea, but he'd insisted he had it covered.

Fuck, she prayed whatever he'd done to save the alpha's life was enough. Otherwise, they were both dead.

A large male with a Herculean body stood from a nearby wooden stool. The stool scraped across the hardwood floor, though she barely heard the noise over the bass thumping in the background. His gunmetal blue eyes flicked between her and Gray. The male strode forward and pointed at them. "You can stay, but your bitch has to go."

Bitch? Where the fuck did this guy get off calling her a bitch? He didn't even know her. Lia opened her mouth, but before she could say anything, Gray intervened. "She stays with me," he declared.

The male's jaw clenched as he lumbered in their direction. Gray shifted her so she stood behind him. Although the male with dirty blond hair had a couple of inches on Gray, he didn't quite tower over them. "You've got a lot of nerve bringing her in here with you."

Gray drew himself up to his full height of six feet two inches, thrust his sharp chin, and stared at the male as if challenging him to start something. "Plymouth," he uttered matter-of-factly. Like that one word resolved the entire situation.

The blond threw his head back in laughter and clapped Gray on the shoulder. "Steel balls," he drawled. With a snort, he dipped his chin at Lia. "What'd you tell her about me?"

"Only what she needed to know." Gray stepped aside. "Lia, this is Herak, alpha of the Moonlit Devils pack. Herak, this is my old lady, Lia."

"A pleasure, I think," she stated as her shoulders sagged in relief. What the hell else could she say? Because sure as shit, she didn't understand what the fuck just transpired between them. Although it seemed the alpha no longer had any interest in killing her.

"I'm sure," Herak replied. "Let's talk." He nodded toward a booth in the back as everyone around them returned to whatever they were doing. A couple of males focused on their game of pool, while a few others turned their attention to the TV affixed to the wall.

Her gaze flipped to Gray, who uttered nothing. He just took her hand in his own, laced their fingers together, and led her after Herak. She'd request an explanation, but with these ears around, it seemed unlikely she'd get one. As they walked toward the back, she surveyed the other bar occupants. Despite the ten males lurking around, she identified only four of them as shapeshifters. Which meant the rest were likely kin. They'd spoken too freely for them to be human.

Herak slipped into one side of the booth while she and Gray took the other with her on the inside. Did he expect her to run? Even if she attempted it, she wouldn't get far. Besides, whether she liked it or not, she still needed his help. So what if it came as a shapeshifter pack? She couldn't do this alone.

"What are we talking?" Herak asked.

"Full-blown protection. For her at a meeting. You'll take the low ground and I'll take the high."

Her head jerked in Gray's direction. "You can't be serious?" They hadn't even discussed the full logistics of the meeting. Nor had she mentioned her suspicions regarding Nina's request.

Gray adjusted in the booth, angling his body toward hers, and draped an arm across the leather cushion. "I can handle hand-to-hand, but I don't know what your sister is capable of. I'll be more useful taking the higher ground."

"And put his entire pack in danger," she stated point blank. "I won't do that. Not even to protect myself." Not to mention she didn't know if her sister had already sold her out.

Herak's eyebrows furrowed as his nose wrinkled. His fingers drummed on the table. "Explain."

Yeah, the male owed Gray a boon, but he deserved all the information. It was the only way to make an informed decision. Regardless of her objection, she couldn't make it for him. Lia glanced around the room. As much as she preferred not to share her history so openly, she didn't have another choice. Letting out a soft sigh, she leaned back. "I don't believe my sister wants to meet for an exchange. I believe my family will be there so they can strip me of my powers."

"Strip your powers?" Gray blinked. "I don't understand. Why would they do that?"

"We don't exactly see eye-to-eye." They hadn't in nearly ten years. She glanced between Gray and Herak. Both males had confusion written all over their faces. Whether she wanted to or not, she had to explain everything. "I went on my first solo hunt at sixteen. Against a vampire. I nearly had him when I got distracted. The guy had a gun pointed at me and another vampire intervened. He saved me. It made me question everything my parents raised me to believe. Hunting the supernatural no longer seemed like the right thing to do. My family didn't like that, so they disowned me, but they didn't strip me of my powers back then. I don't know if vampires, shapeshifters, or witches can have that happen, but hunters can. The only thing that makes sense...something in the supernatural world has shifted. Since my family doesn't see me as someone on their side, I'm the enemy. The only way to make me vulnerable is to take my powers."

Herak scrubbed a hand across his face. "How many hunters are we talking about here?"

That was a damn good question. One she wasn't entirely sure she had the answer to, but she'd do her best. It would take her immediate family to execute a power strip. She'd only ever read about it, never witnessed it. "Five, at the least. My sister, two brothers, and parents. If they include extended family, it could be ten or more." None of that accounted for Nina selling the drive or turning it over. That seemed unlikely. Especially if they planned to strip her powers.

"There's something else, isn't there?" Gray posed, ripping her from her thoughts.

"Possibly. It just...it serves no purpose." None that she could come up with, anyway.

"What is it?"

"Nina could've disclosed information regarding the meeting to The Grim Reaper. We might have to account for his men, too." Better to get it all out there. Then they could prepare for every possibility.

Herak's dark eyes scoured the room and then returned to them. "This isn't a small ask, Gray. Even repayment for a life goes so far."

Dipping his chin, he acknowledged the male's response, squeezed Lia's shoulder, and focused his gaze on Harek. "Then name your price."

"Twenty."

"Done."

The two males shook hands. Her eyes widened. Was he serious? He couldn't mean it. She'd already made it clear she didn't have money. Not like this. All the cash she possessed sat in her bag. She couldn't pay for protection.

"I'll get the treasurer and we'll finalize arrangements." Harek climbed out of the booth.

Lia waited until the male was out of earshot. "What are you doing? I can't afford that."

"I'm paying." Gray caressed her cheek with the back of his knuckles. "I thought I made it clear...your safety is all that matters to me."

Despite how many times he'd said it, she hadn't fully believed it. They'd known one another for a day. How could he care so much about her already? It made no sense, but then again, maybe it didn't have to. There was a lot she couldn't explain regarding him. Why he felt so protective of her...or why she couldn't just walk away. Wrapping a hand around the back of his neck, Lia brushed a tender kiss across his lips. "Thank you."

"I'd say it's unnecessary, but..." his words trailed off. Not that she needed him to finish the statement. The corner of his mouth lifted into a lopsided grin. "Text your sister. Let's get things in motion."

Lia nodded. She dug out Otis's cell and shot a text off to her sister. With the location and time chosen, they'd planned for every scenario. Or so she hoped.

From his high perch atop the roof of the building across from the warehouse, Gray monitored everything happening below. They had three wireless earpieces between them. Both he and Lia had one, as did Harek. The male had some kind of telepathic communication with his pack, so it worked out best for all involved. Through the scope of his rifle, he eyed Lia, who stood there with a briefcase in hand. It contained counterfeit bills.

Another thing Harek had provided. For an additional ten grand. Money well spent if all of this kept Lia safe. It wasn't as if he'd spent much of all he'd earned over the years, outside of the normal anyway. His apartment he always paid for in advance. And the weapons he stored in multiple places across the world, including secluded caverns throughout the Atlantic.

"She's late," Lia mumbled.

"Let's not dip out just yet," Gray replied. Harek's pack had chosen their hiding places well. If they moved too soon, it could give each member's position away, and they'd lose their advantage.

"Agreed," Harek echoed.

Gray scanned the cracked pavement of the empty lot, searching for something approaching their location. Either by foot or—a black nondescript sedan turned into the lot. He studied it through the scope, but couldn't gather much regarding the details. "Heads up. Vehicle coming in."

"Is it her?"

"I can't tell. It's got tinted windows." Which meant it had to be Nina, right? Who else would've driven out to an abandoned warehouse? Unless Lia was right. Not that he could tell until they parked.

The car stopped near the delivery bay. Lia didn't move from her spot by a stack of empty pallets. The corrugated metal door remained open, so whomever drove the sedan could easily see inside the warehouse. As much as they wanted them to, anyway. A woman with blue-black hair climbed out of the vehicle and marched toward Lia.

"I was beginning to think you flaked on our deal," Lia called out.

That answered that question. The female who'd arrived was Nina. Thus far, she appeared to have shown up alone. A jittery sensation in his belly suggested otherwise. Gray inhaled and exhaled a deep breath, focusing on what he saw below. His woman needed him in a state of calm. Her survival depended on it.

"Of course not, dear sister. I just wanted to ensure everything was in place," Nina replied as she stopped in front of the sedan.

Lia's gaze zeroed in on the dark-haired female. "Meaning what? This isn't anything more than an exchange."

"Yet we haven't seen one another in over ten years. Why skip all the pleasantries?"

"What pleasantries?" Lia scoffed. "You and everyone else in our family turned their backs on me. Am I just supposed to forget all of that? Act like none of it happened?"

"Something like that."

His woman rubbed her thumb across her brow and shook her head as she clutched the briefcase's handle. "What is this, Nina? Because sure as shit, it doesn't seem like you're here to collect money and return my property."

Striding forward, Nina closed the distance between to the two of them. "I'm here to give you an opportunity. To walk away from the life you've led and come back to the fold."

"Excuse me? What the fuck are you prattling on about?"

"It's quite simple, really. I'll give you the names of a couple of vampires to dispose of, and if you succeed, we'll welcome you home."

Gray frowned. What the fuck was this? Certainly not something they'd anticipated. Lia had made it clear earlier that her family wanted nothing to do with her. Given what Nina mentioned about the time apart...why would that have changed? Unless...

"Company," Herak's voice came across their communication device.

Shit. Through the scope, Gray adjusted his sights to the backside of the warehouse. Two more black sedans with tinted windows turned in. They had a minute, maybe two, before chaos unfolded. He focused back on his woman. "She's stalling."

Shifting the briefcase to one hand, Lia pulled a 9MM Sig Sauer from the small of her back and aimed it at Nina. "What the fuck did you do?"

Holy shit. Was that *his* gun? Had she found one of his secret compartments? "You little minx," Gray muttered. As much as it impressed him, it also irritated him. She shouldn't have gotten into his things so easily.

"What I had to." Nina smirked. "We couldn't risk the help you'd give them."

The three doors of the sedan parked in front of the warehouse opened. Four more people climbed out of it—three males and one female. "Natalia!" the female hollered.

"Mom?" Lia said as her gaze flicked to the female standing by the backseat passenger door.

Nina surged forward, reaching for the gun in Lia's hand. Not that Lia let go of it. The two struggled, each attempting to gain control. Before Gray could suggest anything, Lia swung the briefcase and forced Nina to leap backward. A shot rang out, the noise bouncing off the walls.

Fuck. What the hell happened? Had Lia gotten hit? His chest tightened as he scrutinized her entire body. Nothing. He didn't—

"Son of a bitch!" Nina screamed, clutching her upper thigh. Blood seeped through her pants and fingers. "You shot me!"

Lia tossed the briefcase aside and aimed the 9MM at her sister. "The next one won't miss."

Shifting his sight to the sedans in the back, he spotted four familiar goons get out of the vehicles with another four he didn't recognize. A second ago, they might've had another way out of this. Now, they only had one choice. "Get her out of here, Herak," Gray snapped as he pulled the trigger, dropping the first of many bodies.

Chapter Five

Lia paced back and forth in front of the bar. Her stilettos clicked against the hardwood floor with each step she took. Attempting to release the tension in her body, she gripped her shoulders tightly. How had everything so quickly gone to shit? They'd prepared for *every* possibility. Well, almost all of them. Although she'd brought the gun along, it hadn't occurred to her she'd actually use it. Even if it was accidental. The last minutes of her so-called exchange with her sister replayed in her mind.

"Natalia!" her mother hollered. The woman's mouth slackened as she shook her head.

"Mom?" Lia said as her gaze flicked to her mother standing by the backseat passenger door. It shouldn't have surprised her that her family hid inside the sedan. But if they planned to strip her powers, why wait? Why hadn't they all exited the vehicle when her sister had?

Nina surged forward, reaching for the gun in Lia's hand. Not that she'd let it go. That wasn't fucking happening. The two of them struggled for control of the weapon. This bitch! Tightening her grip on the 9MM, she swung the briefcase and forced her sister to leap backward. A shot rang out, echoing off the walls.

"Son of a bitch!" her sister screamed, clutching her upper thigh. Blood seeped through the cotton material of Nina's pants, pooling beneath her fingers. "You shot me!"

Shit! She hadn't meant to pull the trigger. Her finger must've slipped. It was the only thing that made sense. That didn't mean she couldn't play this off to her advantage, especially with her entire family standing there gawking at her. Lia tossed the briefcase aside and aimed the Sig Sauer at her sister. "The next one won't miss."

"Get her out of here, Herak," Gray snapped across their communication devices.

What? No. Fuck. Had something...wait, Herak had mentioned company a couple of minutes ago. Her sister had done something. She figured that much out. "Where's the drive?" Lia yelled.

"Where it belongs." Nina's upper lip curled. "With The Grim Reaper."

The muffled sounds of car doors opening and shutting came from somewhere behind her. Shit. Either more of her family just showed up or—a thud resounded from the back of the warehouse. Garbled shouts followed it. Not that she could make out any of the words, nor could she look. Fuck. Lia took a step backward.

"Right on time," her sister said.

Out of her periphery, she caught movement around the car. Her father reached for Nina just as the flash of a muzzle went off, someone knocked her down and they skidded across the ground. Lia grunted as her back hit the concrete. "Ow," she bit out, though she was grateful they'd gotten her out of the way. Her gaze flipped to the large, red-headed male on top of her. Crimson stained the shirt he had on under his leather jacket. "You're hit."

"Tis nothin'. Now, we've got to go."

"No!" She didn't want to leave without Gray. They couldn't. Especially not with her family brandishing weapons. Sure as fuck, that shot had come from one of her brothers.

Without another word, Oren scrambled to his feet, scooped her up, and tossed her over his shoulder.

"Damn it! Put me down!" Lia barked. Her words fell on deaf ears. Oren darted toward a door. As she pounded on his back, she glimpsed a blaze of fire striking the ground near her family's sedan. If nothing else, at least they couldn't follow them.

"Pacing isn't gonna help," Herak said. He peered over his shoulder at her as he wiped the blood from his hands on a towel. "Good call on the anti-venin."

"Yeah, well, I expected my family might use weapons. Rare, but...we make our bullets. Silver and copper combination." God, she hated this. "Where the fuck is he?" Gray should've returned by now. Nearly an hour had passed since the shifters had brought her back to their club.

"Clean up takes time. The last thing we need is for humans to stumble upon whatever mess got left behind."

Mess? What could he have had to clean? All right. Whoever had shown up to help her family. Those assholes. Although her family tried to kill her, she hoped they'd gotten out alive. Maybe a little worse for wear, just not dead. Lia swept her dark tresses over her shoulder. "I need a fucking drink. Waiting sucks. How can you just sit there?"

Herak smirked. "He paid me for a job, not to worry over whether he'd make it back in one piece."

Lia halted in her tracks as she clenched her jaw. Right. *The job.* The one that focused on protecting her. She opened her mouth—the door flung open and

Gray waltzed in with a bag slung over his shoulder. Without a single word, Lia darted across the room and threw her arms around him. "You're alive." She didn't give a shit about the bag biting into her flesh. He was okay, and that was all she cared about.

"Of course I am." Gray pulled back a touch and brushed the backs of his knuckles across her cheek. "Did you expect otherwise?"

No. It didn't mean she hadn't worried like crazy that something had gone wrong. Though she didn't want to say all of that because it was crazy. They hardly knew one another. Fuck, she shouldn't have even flung herself at him. "I just...I figured you'd be right behind us," she admitted. That much wouldn't hurt, right?

"My apologies. I didn't mean to take so long." He pressed a tender kiss to her forehead. "There is something we need to discuss. Privately."

"Sure. Why not?" Herak let out an exasperated sigh. "Take a room down the hall. First door on the left is open."

That didn't sound comforting. Or maybe the male had tired of providing them hospitality. Though Gray paid him for part of his help, the male had done a lot for them. Releasing his hold on her, Gray dipped his chin at Herak and led her around the bar. They rounded the corner, heading down the hallway, and disappeared into a nearby bedroom.

Lia surveyed the room as Gray shut the door. Despite the dark blue curtains that matched the queen-sized bed's comforter, there wasn't much in the way of décor. A single landscape painting of a forest hung on the wall. Guess shapeshifters required little regarding a room. She glanced over her shoulder. "What's so important we couldn't discuss it in front of the pack?"

Letting out a heavy breath, he set the bag down, dropped his hands to his hips, and stared at her. "Do you know The Grim Reaper's real name?"

That was a strange question. Her eyebrows pinched together as she faced him. "Of course I do."

"Ilario Scamardo?"

What the fuck? "How'd you know that?" Not once had she ever mentioned him by name. For a damn good reason. Just because she'd needed his help hadn't meant she was prepared to share everything. Something that had somehow changed over the last two days. She'd worry about that later. Right now, she needed an explanation.

Gray gripped the back of his neck and paced back and forth across the bedroom. Silence stretched between them.

What the hell was she supposed to do in this situation? At no point in her twenty-five years had she gotten close to anyone. Yeah, they'd talked about some real shit. Things she hadn't shared with any of her friends. Not that she had any real ones or someone she actually cared about. Except for maybe him. Stepping forward, Lia grabbed a hold of his arm and stopped his pacing. "Please, just talk to me."

"I'm not who you think I am." He sighed. "Or even what you think."

"Which means what, exactly?" She'd already figured out he was supernatural of some kind. Especially given some of his connections. And his lack of reaction to the information that mythological creatures existed, along with what she'd told him regarding vampires, only confirmed that suspicion.

"I knew Ilario in another life. He's the reason I am what I am." His gaze met hers as he dragged a hand through his hair. "Twenty years ago, I disobeyed an order he gave me. He had me killed, but I was reborn."

Nothing about that made sense. She shook her head. "You're not a vampire. I'd know." Plus, he hadn't known how to kill them.

"You're right." His midnight blue eyes focused on hers. "I'm a merman."

Gray leaned against the wall, draped one ankle over the other, and folded his arm across his chest. Three words that had never left his mouth before. Not since the day he'd turned. A day he hadn't forgotten or thought about in twenty years. Even with all the work he'd done for the pod, that day hadn't crossed his mind.

Taking a few steps back, Lia slowly dropped onto the bed. She let out a short laugh and ran her hands through her hair, pulling it from her shoulders.

Maybe he should say something, but what? How could he ease whatever thoughts pummeled his woman's brain? Hopefully, his leader didn't find out about this. Though he suspected Lia wasn't the first landwalker to learn of their existence. At least purposely.

Her gaze dropped to the floor. "I'm sorry, I'm just...trying to wrap my head around this." She shook her head. "I mean...everything I thought I knew is basically bullshit."

"That isn't entirely true. You simply learned a new...facet. That's all." Just as he had a couple of days ago. He'd always known things beyond mermaids possibly existed, just without proof. Something he'd discovered twenty years earlier. "We all come from somewhere, right?"

"Yeah, I guess." Her honey-brown eyes lifted to him as she leaned forward, pressing her elbows into her thighs. "You said you disobeyed an order. What exactly did you do for him?"

Gray scrubbed a hand across his face. It shouldn't have surprised him she asked, though he'd hoped to avoid this part of the conversation. "I handled a...certain kind of contract, except women and children. That hasn't ever changed. Ilario knew this, and he sent me after a fifteen-year-old boy. I refused. We spoke in his office at length and I thought...we'd come to an understanding."

That had been the furthest from the truth.

"Where do you think you're going?" Ilario asked.

Gray stopped mid-turn and peered at the male. He didn't like the tone Ilario had taken, but he'd overlook it. "We've come to an agreement. Our conversation is finished."

The man's upper lip curled off his teeth. "Is that what you think?" Clasping his hands at the small of his back, Ilario took a couple of steps forward. "Things are done when I say they are. While we have discussed this ad nauseam, the only thing finished here...is you."

"Excuse me?" No way did the male have the balls to take him out. Even without his weapons, he was still deadly. Though it wouldn't be wise to attack too fast. He'd have the whole family after him.

"Allow me to put this into words you'll understand," Ilario stated. "Your services are no longer required."

The double set of oak doors opened. Four large men entered, stopping just inside the doorway. They must've expected he'd make it easy on them. Gray balled up his fist and threw an uppercut that landed hard against Ilario's jaw, knocking the male into the large oak desk not ten feet back.

Three of the men surged forward. Gray dodged the first punch, side-kicked one guard, and parried another attack. Something sharp pricked him in the neck. Brushing off the slight sting, he leaped toward one male, evaded a throat punch, got behind the guy, and tightly wrapped his arm around his neck. With a hard jerk, the guard crumbled to the ground.

Gray stumbled backward. He tried to shake off the onslaught of lightheadedness, but it came on strong. Shit. Someone must've hit him with a drug. Despite every effort he made, the darkness claimed him and he fell to the floor.

"But you didn't?" Lia's voice interrupted the memory. "Did you?"

"No."

"So...if you were...human once, how did..." she gestured to him. "This happen?"

The inevitable question. How much did he explain to her? He'd already given her more than he ever expected. Not that he'd planned on all that had happened. With what brewed in his mind, it was best if he told her all he could.

"Magic. At least some form of it." A faint smirk crossed his face. "They threw me into the Hudson. Just like they did with you." He recounted part of what he remembered from that day.

Air filled his lungs. Slowly, his eyes opened. Deep blue water surrounded him. What the fuck? How was he breathing? How was he...his gaze jerked all around him. The last thing he recalled, he'd struggled against the rope around his wrists and ankles. None of it was there.

"Be of ease. You're safe," a feminine voice stated.

His eyes fell on the dark-haired female in front of him. He completely drank her in. His eyes widened as he spotted the tail she sported. "What the fuck?" Gray fishtailed backward.

"If you leave, you won't survive!" she called after him.

He halted and peered back at her. "What the fuck did you do to me?"

"I don't understand. How did you become...this? A merman." Lia propped an arm behind her. "Because you kissed me, and that sure as fuck didn't happen to me."

"No, it didn't. I kissed you to give you air, which was only temporary. The transformation is...painful. I'd never wish it on anyone." He paused. Not once had he ever shared this before. He hadn't even spoken her name since the day she died. "The mermaid who saved me...Sharra...she kissed me to give me a chance. All because I'd unknowingly protected her. It was our leader who gave me a new life at her behest."

With each word he uttered, Lia sat up on the bed. "How did you even know I was there? That they threw me into the water?"

"The right place at the right time." It seemed like an oversimplified explanation, but it was the truth. "I do whatever I can to protect our waters. One of your attackers, he was among a group on a boat that dumped oil drums. I hunted—"

"The other four," she said, cutting him off. "They were all Ilario's men. Those drums...it was just among a multitude of shipments he's ordered thrown into the Atlantic."

Gray pushed off the wall and eyed her. Whether she'd intended, she'd given him all the ammunition he needed to fully go after Ilario. To fully dispose of that male for good. "How do you know that?"

"It's part of the information I've spent the last five years collecting on Ilario's activities. Everything I needed to expose him and his deeds."

The drive she'd gone after with desperation. With what he knew now, exposure wasn't enough. His jaw clenched. Not nearly enough. "Then you understand why I need to deal with him."

"Deal with him, how, Gray?" She jumped to her feet. "Because if you're thinking of just taking him out, it won't be easy."

"I know his compound. You just be a good girl and stay here, pet. Harek will keep you safe." It was his place to handle the rest. He turned toward the door.

"Fuck you!" Lia grabbed his arm and yanked him back, glaring at him. "No fucking way are you going without me! You don't know shit regarding his place."

His gaze flicked to the hold she had on his biceps as his entire body tensed. No one had ever dared to stop him like this or defy him as much as she did. While it annoyed him, it also aroused him. "I worked for the male for years and helped establish his security protocols. If anyone knows anything, it's me."

"Really?" Cocking a hip out, she crossed her arms and narrowed her honey-brown eyes at him. "You know about the bulletproof glass? And all the supernatural beings on his staff?"

Fuck. She had a point. Technology had advanced a lot over the last twenty years. It only made sense Ilario would've upgraded along the way. That must've been how she'd gotten involved. Gray gripped the back of his neck. "Fine. But you provide intel only. Do you understand me?"

"How do you think that's going to work? Even if I share all that I know, there's still no way you get in alone. Object until you're blue in the face, but eventually you'll have to relinquish and admit that you need me."

That was the problem. He needed her...alive. Not fighting at his side. The warehouse was a unique situation. Her sister expected her. He couldn't have gotten around that if he tried. Gray closed the distance between them and cupped her cheek. "Do you even get how important you are to me, Lia? What you mean to me?"

Her gaze met his as she leaned into his touch. "And you don't think you matter to me? As insane as it fucking is and I can't explain, I'll do whatever it takes to have your back."

"Like digging into my personal space and stealing a gun?" He smirked, though he didn't fault her for bringing it. And she'd used it without blinking an eye. Even if it was an accident.

"Hey, you gave me the chance to snoop." She cracked a grin, stepped into him, and brushed a tender kiss across his lips. "So you can't blame me for that."

A low rumble sounded in his chest. Shit. He really liked when she did that. "Though I enjoy you trying, you won't change my mind."

"Really? Then think about this. Even with all the details of his compound and security, you won't just need others to help with the rogues, you'll need a distraction."

Other supernaturals. He could bring Harek's pack with him. They'd help defeat rogues. While he usually worked from a distance, he could fight hand-to-hand, he'd just need better equipment. Still, there were only six of them. Maybe Harek could get a message out to the other packs. That could cause delays and give Ilario a chance to increase security. None of which included his own time limits. His heart thudded dully in his chest. He couldn't come up with a single solution that didn't include her. Gray let out a heavy sigh. If they had to work together for him to keep her safe, then that's what they'd do. "All right. Tell me your plan."

Chapter Six

Lia groaned as she cracked an eye open. Fuck. It was too damn early in the morning to get up and moving, but they had things to do. They'd spent most of last night pulling everything together for their plan. Yes, it gave Ilario time to bolster security, but she'd accounted for that. As long as everything went off without a hitch, they should all walk away from this in one piece. She stretched her legs out.

Gray's arm tightened around her mid-section, tugging her closer. "Not yet. Just a little longer."

His erection pressed slightly against her ass. She barely bit back a moan as warmth speared the junction between her thighs. With the amount of times they'd come together over the last couple of days, she really shouldn't want him again. Truthfully, no matter how much they prepared, one or both of them could die today. Not that she wanted to think about that extremely real possibility. Lia glanced over her shoulder at him.

Maybe they could both do with a brief distraction. She pushed her ass back, rubbing it against his shaft.

"If you keep that up, we're not getting out of bed anytime soon," he growled in her ear.

"Would that be a bad thing?" she whispered huskily.

"By the look in your eyes...not entirely." Gray tucked a strand of her hair back. "Where'd your head go?"

Gods, she didn't want to answer that. It had gone nowhere good. Lia opened her mouth and snapped it shut. Though she wanted to tell him anything but the truth, she couldn't. "Just everything that could happen."

"Then let's go over the plan again."

"Every detail?" She cocked an eyebrow at him. That seemed extreme. Even if it would settle her nerves, they'd covered it from top to bottom last night.

"Let's do an overview." He pressed a soft kiss to her shoulder. "There's nothing wrong with being cautious."

Yeah, she supposed there wasn't. It couldn't hurt to review it all again. "Ruby and Rain have four initial explosions set. Three will go off simultaneously. One in the front, one in the back, and one via the sewer access, which will let us in. The fourth will go off once we're inside, separating his forces. Half of the pack will attack the back and the other half will attack the front while we make our way toward Ilario's office. We've got two sharpshooters picking off stragglers." They'd all agreed no one could escape the complex. After they'd dealt with Ilario and his men, the twin witches would destroy the compound. They'd leave nothing but rubble in their wake.

"And you trust Ruby and Rain to handle their part, right?"

"Yes." After what she'd done for them, those two females owed her more than their lives. She'd even asked them to teach Otis a lesson. Something they'd eagerly agreed to do. "And the sharpshooters? Do you trust them?" Both were contacts of Harek's. Despite how much time Gray had spent in New York City over the years, the male had limited resources. At least not without tapping into his watery connections. Neither of them believed that was necessary.

"I do." He caressed her cheek with the backs of his knuckles. "I know there are things that can go wrong, but I promise you I won't let anything happen to you."

"Or you?" Because she couldn't fathom a life without him. They'd known one another all of three days, yet she felt more connected to him than anyone else in her life.

"I'll do everything in my power to ensure we both come out the other side."

Their gazes met and held. She wrapped a hand around the back of his neck, slid her fingers through his silky locks, and fused her lips to his. His words meant more than she could describe. It wasn't enough to just tell him how much she believed him. She needed to show him.

Deepening the kiss, his fingers trailed over the curve of her ass and between her thighs. Gray ran his digits across her slit and dipped his fingers within the folds of her pussy. Slowly driving them in and out of her, he claimed her body all over again.

Lia moaned into the kiss. Fuck, he knew just how to drive her crazy. She shifted a knee, moving her leg to open up more, as she rocked back against his fingers and rubbed her ass against his shaft. The friction between them, plus the sheets covering their bodies, intensified the way every synapse lit up. Jolts of heat shot to her core.

Her taste buds hummed with his succulent taste. As their tongues entangled, she memorized every inch of his mouth. She didn't want to forget any perfect part of him. As if he couldn't wait any longer, he removed his fingers from her pussy and eased his cock deep inside of her. With one slow thrust after another, Gray drove into her until she fully sheathed him.

His fingertips traced over her hip as his arm came around her waist. Her hand found his and their fingers laced together as he pistoned in and out of her. She rocked her hips back, meeting each of his thrusts. Each stroke of his cock drove her higher, sending a spark of electricity surging across every nerve-ending in her body.

The grip she had in his hair tightened. Regardless of the number of times they'd already come together, this felt different. Special. There was just something about him. Something she couldn't pinpoint or explain. Maybe she didn't have to. Not when he continuously took her breath away. In a moment like this, understanding why didn't matter all that much.

It was like they expressed everything they couldn't admit to one another with their bodies. As if they could say what they didn't dare openly utter. That if things went wrong, at least the two of them had this moment to add to all the other beautiful memories they shared. That everything they had together mattered.

His fingers clamped around hers as he drove into her faster and harder. Her thighs clenched as the inferno in her core erupted. The kiss broke off. They both cried out in ecstasy. A massive orgasm detonated inside of her at the same time one exploded out of him, drenching their thighs. Neither of them stilled until they'd worked through their mutual release.

Gray and Lia stared at one another. His midnight blue eyes sparkled brighter than she'd ever seen before. It was almost like she could see the expansive ocean in his eyes. Nothing had ever looked so stunning.

Through ragged breaths, he brushed a tender kiss across her lips and pressed his forehead to hers. Without a word, he slipped out of her and climbed out of the bed.

And just like that, whatever moment they'd shared was over. Not that she could think about that right then. They had too much at stake to focus on anything other than the battle ahead.

Gray surveyed the filth-encrusted wall the beam of his flashlight played off of as they slowed their pace. If Lia noticed the cold water that sloshed beneath their footsteps, she said nothing. Not that she'd spoken much since this morning. Then again, neither had he. Even as he'd watched her strap a myriad of weapons across her person, silence stretched between them. Which perplexed him a bit. After what happened, he'd expected...something.

As they halted in their tracks, Lia pointed to the access point about ten feet ahead. "That's where we're going up."

The stench of stagnant, dirty water slammed into him. What the fuck had these animals done to cause such an odor? He balled his hands into fists, though it did little to release the tension in his body. "So, why are we stopping?"

Lia glanced at the time on her watch. "Because we're about...sixty seconds early."

Only sixty? Shit, he thought they'd arrived right on schedule. Getting through the sewer system was the simple part. The rats they'd encountered hadn't bothered him. All the debris he'd noticed along their route had. Now, he was beyond ready to obliterate anyone who stood between him and an enemy he should've taken out years ago.

Gray rolled his neck. His gaze fell on Lia. They had a few seconds before things went off. Maybe now he could address what happened this morning. He wanted...no, needed her to be careful. He drank her in from head to toe. She had matching guns holstered at chest level. They each contained handmade bullets comprising silver and copper shavings. Then the 9MM Sig Sauer he'd returned to her. She'd holstered it at the small of her back. He liked that she had his weapon on her person. That didn't include the silver and copper daggers strapped to each of her thighs, along with a few other steel blades he'd watched her discreetly hide in her boots and beltline. With all of that weaponry at her disposal, she'd make it out. But he needed her to know how much she meant to him. "Hey, Lia—" Gray started.

A loud boom echoed around them as a metal grate hit the ground just beneath the access point ahead. Water and dirt kicked up around it. Lia glanced at him. "That's our queue."

He grabbed her arm, curling his fingers around the crook of her elbow. "Can you just wait two seconds?" Because he needed to get this out. The moment between them in his bed earlier scared the shit out of him. Staring into her eyes like that, he'd realized how much he actually had to lose. What he felt for her...he'd never experienced it before. Not even with the mermaid who saved his life. As she looked at him with those exquisite honey-brown eyes of hers, he still couldn't find the words to say. Gray swallowed the lump in his throat, cupped her jaw, and brushed his thumb across her cheek. "Don't do anything stupid."

Covering his hand with her own, she leaned into his touch. "Don't do anything heroic."

The corner of his mouth curled as he pressed a soft kiss to her lips. Yeah. They didn't require any of that fluffy shit to express their emotions. "Let's go."

Lia cracked a smile and took off toward the access point. Tucking away his flashlight, he followed her. With him right behind her, they climbed the ladder. It creaked slightly under their weight, likely a result of the explosion. Still, it held as they made their way to the top. "We're almost there," Lia whispered.

They'd agreed for her to go first since she had better eyesight. He had equipment to use in the surrounding darkness, but she didn't require any of that. So, he kept hot on her tail as they ascended the ladder. As his fingers came around the next rung, his eyes adjusted to the lack of light.

Lia stopped. A slight grunt left her mouth as she hefted a floor panel above her head and pushed it aside. She climbed up the rest of the way, him right behind her. Gray peered around the room. Bright lights lined the floor of each wall. With the lights on all the machines, it wasn't really necessary. They'd gotten into the electrical room.

"You gonna stand there all day or show me something?" Lia smirked.

Oh, he had something to show her, all right. Just nothing like what popped into his mind right then. That was later. Gray cracked his knuckles, strode over to the nearest grid, placed his hands on the cool metal, and let his power do the rest. His fingers sparked and crackled as waves of electricity shot out of him, surging through the equipment like it was nothing. The machine popped and smoked. Fuck. He rather enjoyed that.

Darkness swallowed them as an alarm blared loudly around the room. Smaller lights along the ceiling clicked on. "That's the backup generator," Lia commented. "We need to move."

He dipped his chin, acknowledging her statement. They'd accomplished their first task. Now they had to get to Ilario. Gray grabbed the hilt of the steel blade sheathed at his hip as he trailed behind her. Together, they slipped into the empty hallway. While anyone they came across may not recognize him, they'd know her.

A sound of footsteps pounding against the floor echoed in the hall just ahead of them. He darted forward and shoved his knife into the male's jugular. Blood spurted everywhere as he yanked it out and the body crumpled to the floor. Out of his periphery, he spotted Lia dispatching another guard. Leaving the dead bodies where they lay, they nodded to one another and continued on.

Together, Gray and Lia rounded a corner and ran right into four more soldiers. Neither of them hesitated. Leaping forward, he impaled one man with the sharp-edged blade and drove it through the guy's chin. As the male collapsed, Gray spun around and kicked another, knocking the guard backward. The other two jumped into action. Not that Lia gave them much wiggle room.

Thumps and thwacks resounded around him as he focused on the one who surged toward him. He didn't want to draw unnecessary attention, so he avoided his gun for the moment. Instead, he reached for another knife and threw it. The male tried, but failed, to dodge it. With a thunk, it embedded in the guy's forehead. Gray glanced at Lia just as she sliced her second attacker's throat. If he hadn't seen it, he wouldn't even notice the blood splatter that covered her black pleather top and pants.

Though he tried, he couldn't stop the low rumble that resounded in his chest. "You've never looked sexier than you do right now."

A sparkle danced in her honey-brown eyes as they hooded. "After all of this is over, I'm gonna fuck your brains out."

"I can't wait." But they had things to handle first. He yanked the knife from the guy's head as they passed by and stalked forward. He peered at her out of his periphery as they headed down the empty hallway toward Ilario's office. "Can you hear anything happening outside?"

"My hearing isn't that good, but I think they've made it inside. There's a lot of commotion at both ends of the compound."

Unlike the last time where they had those communication devices, they'd opted for radio silence. With the explosions that had gotten rigged, it seemed the best option. He hoped that proved accurate.

They didn't encounter any others as they headed to Ilario's office. Lia eyed him and removed the Sig Sauer from the small of her back, holding it by her leg. Despite those they'd already killed, they expected more than just humans on the other side. With a slight nod, he dug out the 45 he carried and a silver-coated dagger.

Wrapping her hand around the doorknob, Lia slowly turned it. As one half of the double-doors silently swung open, Gray pressed his back against the other. He surveyed the office he hadn't seen in two decades. Nothing appeared out of the ordinary, though he couldn't see everything from this angle. Only the chair that sat in the corner near the window. With his gun out, he stepped just inside the doorframe.

Before he could react, a hand wrapped around his forearm, jerked him forward, and threw him across the office. As he landed on the carpet, both his blade and 45 skittered along the floor. Motherfucker! Gray jumped back to his feet just as a large body slammed into him, knocking him down. It had to be a fucking vampire. Nothing else moved that fast. Not even hunters, according to what Lia had told him.

Which meant he couldn't trust his eyes. The only way he'd catch this fucker was if he focused on all the surrounding sounds. Every little noise, including the birds chirping outside, or how the paper on the oak desk rustled. Curling his fingers around the hilt of a silver blade tucked in his boot, he waited for the right moment. A slight breeze bristled the hair on his arm and then blew back in the opposite direction. As it came around again, Gray sprang to his feet, dodged a hit to the back, spun around, and drove a silver knife into its heart.

As he yanked the blade out, the creature hiccupped blood and flopped backward. A bright orange blaze crackled as it engulfed the vampire, burning the thing until nothing remained. The sound of a hiss drew his attention. Facing the direction of the noise, his gaze landed first on Lia and the male who held a knife to her throat, and then shifted to Ilario, who pointed a gun at him.

"Drop it," Ilario demanded.

Gray clenched his jaw. That fucking piece of shit must've come from the safe room Lia mentioned. As much as they'd prepared for vampires, it didn't seem they'd prepared enough. Not that he'd let this asshole harm either of them. He just had to stall until either Harek arrived or he came up with another plan. As much as it irked him, Gray tossed the dagger to the ground. "If it isn't the weasel of New York City himself. Long time no see."

Ilario tilted his head as his upper lip curled and his dark eyes narrowed. "Didn't I kill you once already? Yeah. Gray Marino. I never forget a face."

"You *thought* you had me killed. Obviously, you failed." From his periphery, he noted the discreet movement of Lia's hand. She had weapons tucked away everywhere. It didn't appear the male who held her even noticed or bothered to search her. That could work to his advantage. A single stab wound and he could take care of the rest. He didn't have to touch his prey to kill them. It was just a preference. Scrutinizing Ilario, Gray smirked. He knew how to get under the male's skin. "Then again, that seems to be your motto lately."

"Maybe, but you and your girl are the ones with weapons pointed in your faces." Ilario glimpsed at Lia. "I should've known the trouble you'd bring. Given the company you're keeping, it was just a matter of time before you ended up on my bad side."

"You have nothing but bad sides, Ilario," Gray stated. "I mean, look at the lengths you had to go to get a tiny ass drive back. Please, don't play stupid. We both know you have it. I can see it in your right pants' pocket." Yeah. Two decades may have gone by, but it seemed some things hadn't changed. Ilario still hated to look like an idiot. Especially in front of his soldiers.

Ilario's head jerked in his direction. The male's nostrils flared. "And you've still got a big mouth. Like I'm gonna let you and this dumb bitch get the best of me."

"We've got company coming, boss."

"Then let's get these two taken care of right this time. No mistakes." Ilario raised the 9MM in his hand and aimed it at Gray.

Lia stabbed her attacker in the thigh. The male screamed as a shot rang out and someone knocked Gray to the ground. It barely registered that Lia had saved him until he noticed how her black blouse darkened. *Shit!* As Gray pressed his palm to her chest, staunching the blood, he lifted his hand and blasted both Ilario and the soldier with a bolt of lightning. Then he threw a continuous stream of electrical volts at them until their bodies crumpled to the floor and smoke billowed from their corpses.

"Sorry," she whispered. "Couldn't let you...die."

"Doesn't mean I'm going to let you do it, either." Gray scooped her into his arms, rose to his full height, and strode toward the door. This shouldn't have fucking happened. Things shouldn't have gone this awry. His breaths burst in and out of his chest. Despite the immense fear that tried to overcome him, he refused to give into it. He had to get Lia out of there and somewhere that could help her. "So don't you fucking give up on me. We're not done yet."

"Think...I...am..." Her words trailed off as she coughed up blood. Her head lolled to the side and her eyes drifted shut.

"Harek!" Gray yelled. The grip he had on her tightened until his knuckles turned white. Not that he gave a shit. He refused to let her go. "Come on, Lia. Stay with me. I've got you. Just stay with me." This wasn't fucking happening. It just couldn't be.

The soft breaths of someone snoring nearby reached her first. A faint beep sounded in her ears. Fuck. What the hell was that noise? It irritated the shit out of her. Lia woke, squinting at the bright light overhead. What the fuck? She turned her head, taking in her surroundings, and flinched at the dull throb in her left shoulder. "Ow," she mumbled. Shit. Somehow, she'd ended up in a hospital. Gods, that wasn't good. Her blood might freak some human out.

"You're awake."

Her gaze shifted toward the soothing sound of Gray's voice. A slow smile settled across his face as he sagged in a well-worn chair. The fog lifted from her mind. The last thing she remembered—she'd knocked him down, taking a shot intended for him. He must've brought her here. What hospital were they at? She recognized nothing in the room. Something to worry about later. At least they were both alive. "Did we get him?"

"Yeah." His midnight blue eyes narrowed at her. "You promised not to do anything stupid."

"You promised not to do anything heroic." They'd both gone back on their promises. Although, now that she thought about it, neither of them promised anything. They'd only made a request of the other. She snickered and winced at the agony that speared through her body. "Don't suppose they're ready to let me go."

"Doubtful," Harek stated from the corner of the room. He stood and stretched his arms above his head. "But I'll check in with Lucian. Give you both a minute alone."

"Thanks," Gray replied. "I appreciate it, man." The two exchanged a look of some kind before Harek exited. Gray leaned forward and refocused on her as he gently stroked the top of her head. "You scared the shit out of me."

"But you didn't die." At that moment, that was all she could think about. Ilario killing him as the vampire killed her. If she had to do it all again, she'd make the same choice. Lia offered him her hand as she noticed the bandage wrapped around his arm.

As he laid his palm on hers, his gaze flicked briefly to his injury. "The bullet went through you and winged me." Gray shook his head. "It barely missed your heart, Lia. You're lucky to be alive. I can't..." He visibly swallowed. "I can't lose you."

The words may have come out softly, but that didn't impact the emotion behind them in the slightest. Whether she'd describe it as love, she couldn't say. But whatever was between them was strong. And something she wanted to grow and hold on to for a very long time. "You won't." She grinned. "Besides, I owe you a fantastic brain fucking, if I recall." Not that she hadn't done that several times already with her exquisite merman. Lia let out a short laugh.

Gray cocked an eyebrow at her. "What's so funny about that?"

"I just realized that...sleeping with the fishes has taken on a whole new meaning."

Despite the way his forehead wrinkled, he shook his head and chuckled. "Never say that again." He brushed a tender kiss across her lips. "Because I'm definitely not a fucking fish."

She giggled and cringed at the pain that lanced her shoulder. "Fuck. Don't make me laugh."

"I can't promise that. Let this serve as a reminder to stay out of trouble while I'm away."

And she couldn't promise that. "Trouble usually finds me. What do you mean 'away'? Where are you going?" Even with all he'd already shared about his kind, they hadn't talked about everything. Something that went both ways.

"As much as I don't want to go, I have to return to sea soon. It's expected and my body requires it, but I'll be back. I always come back."

"Promise?" Maybe all they needed to promise was that they'd figure this out. Though deep down, she already knew they would. No amount of distance would keep them apart. That was the only truth that mattered, yet she still needed to hear it. An actual promise that he'd return to her.

"I swear to you, Natalia Esposito, that I will return. Nothing can keep me away from you."

"Good, because I feel the same way." She'd fight whatever struggle or battle came along. As long as she had him by her side, they'd survive all of it.

Wind rustled the nearby trees. Water splashed as it slapped against a collection of hulls and pylons. Aside from the three of them, the marina was empty this time of night. Gray dropped his gaze to Lia as she ran her fingers across the phoenix on his right arm. "What are you doing?"

"Memorizing every mark." Her honey-brown eyes lifted to his. "Do you have a problem with that?"

She'd done the same thing as they lay in bed this morning. Three days had passed since her time in the hospital. Despite his objections, Lucian had released Lia twenty-four hours after admission. The male insisted that she'd heal nearly as quickly as a shifter. Gray caressed the small scar that lingered where she'd gotten shot. As much as he wanted to stay, he couldn't. It seemed they each had their own way of stalling. "No," he muttered, allowing her to continue tracing each of his tattoos. At least the ones she could reach—ace of clubs on his left forearm, crisscrossed daggers on his right forearm, and a blade stabbed through a skull on his left biceps. Maybe when he got back, he should add another. "Promise me you'll stay out of trouble until I return."

"How long are you gonna be gone again?"

"Look for me on the horizon at the next full moon." Provided his leader permitted his return. Not that he tacked that on. The female rarely declined his requests.

"You realize that's almost two weeks and there are things I need to do, right?"

"I know." He lifted a hand, silencing her before she could interrupt. "Yes, I know everything got handled with Ilario and he's no longer a threat, but that doesn't mean you're safe."

"Which is why Harek is hovering back there like a hawk ready to pounce, and you gave me a key and showed me all your hiding spots in the apartment."

While all of that was true, that didn't mean he wanted her out there searching for trouble. Gray dragged a hand through his hair. Still, he had to convince her to be careful. He cupped her jaw and stroked her cheek with his thumb. Their eyes locked on one another. Determination filled her gaze as her eyebrows furrowed. He let out an exasperated sigh. "Stubborn and sexy. A dangerous package, but one I need. So promise me this. When you go searching for answers, take one of the Moonlit Devils along. At least while I'm not around." They had made her an honorary member.

Grinning widely, Lia pushed up on her tiptoes and pressed a kiss to his lips. "That I can do."

Although the witches had destroyed Ilario's compound, they weren't free from enemies. Lia's family might try something again. Or someone associated with those unnamed vampires her family wanted dead. "Then maybe by the time I get back, you'll have some answers."

"That's the plan."

Gray flicked his gaze to Harek, who stood at the end of the pier. It was strange to have anyone around. Normally, he returned to his pod with no prying eyes, but these were special circumstances. Although he and Lia spent the last few days addressing everything about his species, this gave him a chance to say goodbye. Brushing another tender kiss across her lips and forehead, he wrapped his arms around her. "I love you, Natalia Esposito," Gray murmured in her hair.

"I love you, Gray Marino."

With a heavy sigh, he nodded to Harek. The male dipped his chin, acknowledging the unspoken request. Gray dropped one last kiss to the top of Lia's head. "I need to go."

"I know," she whispered, though she didn't release the hold she had on him.

Yeah, he wasn't ready to let go, either. But he couldn't wait any longer. The sea called out to him. "Time will fly and I'll be back before you know it." Taking her hands in his own, he kissed the top of each and stepped back. Gray unbuttoned the jeans he had on and shoved them down his legs as he got naked. He handed his pants over to her. "The next full moon."

"The next full moon," Lia repeated.

Turning around, he dove into the Hudson. Although he had a way to swim, it never took long for the transition to begin. The cool water washed over him as his muscles jumped under his skin. His neck corded. Pain speared through him as his lower extremities snapped and merged from legs to a tail covered in black shimmering scales.

Strange, Gray thought. Typically, the agony that wracked him drove him farther under the waves. It was the only thing that ever helped with the transition between forms. But this time…he didn't notice it as much. Instead, his memories of Lia replayed in his mind.

Because no matter how much time they had to spend apart, she'd be there waiting for him. They'd cross whatever boundaries necessary to be together. Time, space, species…nothing could separate them. Nothing could take away what they'd discovered. He knew without a doubt they'd always find their way back to one another. That was the beauty of what he had to look toward—a new life that no one could touch.

Gray chuckled as he dove deeper beneath the waves, heading toward his pod. Sharra would laugh if she could see him now. He recalled one of the last things she'd ever said to him.

"Love can change the world. Watch. One day, everything you think you know will be different. All because you fell in love."

She was right. He saw the world a little differently. Love had changed everything for him. And that was beautiful.

The End

NYC World

Although this book can be read as a standalone, if you enjoyed my NYC world, other books are more prominently featured. I have three series altogether. They can be read separately, in series order, or reading order. That probably sounds redundant, but it's not.

There are vampires, shifters, and witches. Oh my! (Yes, I always have a Dorothy moment.) No, the hunters don't get their own book(s), but they make lots of appearances, mostly as the villains.

Every book is a retelling—Shakespeare, fairytale, and Greek myths.

Here's the reading order (if you're so inclined to go that route):

Detached

Grace's Beast

Savage Seas

Shattered Wonderland

The rest I'm sure you can figure out with the links below.

The Midnight Chronicles

The Lucent Chronicles

The Mystic Chronicles

About the author

Author of the Love's Worth Series, **Brigit Rosé**—like the wine, not the flower—lives in a world of romance. She has taken her life experience and made it into one endless love story. When she's not writing, she's singing loudly and off-key, hanging out with friends, or playing with her two fur babies. She can usually be found with a kiss in one hand and a twist of line in the other, exactly the stories she likes to read and write. If you'd like to know more about Brigit, you can find out more on her website: https://kbfennerrose.com

Also by Brigit Rosé

Love's Worth Series
UnHinged
ReIgnited
The Mystic Chronicles
Detached
The Lucent Chronicles
Grace's Beast
The Arcarean Academy
Wicked Ground

Co-Authored

Prisma Isle Series
Perfectly Reckless
Chaotic Tranquility
Rebel Tides
Siren's Curse
Prisma Isle Coloring & Puzzle Book: Volume 1

Under Krys Fenner

Dark Road Series
Addicted
Damaged
Avenged
Burned
Twisted
The Guardhian Series
Awakened
Disillusioned
The Atlis Chronicles
Blood Sacrifice (appears in charity anthology Forgotten Lore)

Coming Soon

Shattered Wonderland (The Lucent Chronicles)
Silencing the Shape Shifter (Prisma Isle Series)
Kingdom of Embers (Prisma Isle Series)
Savage Ground (The Arcarean Academy)
Hunted (The Atlis Chronicles)
Consumed (The Mystic Chronicles)
Inherited (The Guardhian Series)
ReUnited (Love's Worth Series)
Betrayed (Dark Road Series)